KILLING

DARKNESS

Jay Heavner

Canaveral Publishing

I0654547

Killing Darkness

by Jay Heavner

Canaveral Publishing, Cocoa, Florida

Mr. Heavner can be contacted at jay@jayheavner.com

Cover by Fineline Printing, Titusville, Florida

Killing Darkness is the fourth in the Braddock's Gold Series by Jay Heavner - *Braddock's Gold, Hunter's Moon, Fool's Wisdom*, and *Killing Darkness*

Mr. Heavner also has a growing Florida Murder Mystery Series - *Death at Windover, Murder at the Canaveral Dine*r, and *Murder at the Indian River*

To Frances and Bessie

Acknowledgment

Thanks to everyone who helped me with Killing Darkness. To my wife, Vivian, for her encouragement, support, and proofing. A special thanks to JoAnn Peterson and Bill Rowland for editing and suggestions. And my first readers, Marsha and Brian Tressler, Dutch Staggs, and Sharon Foulk. Thanks.

And a special acknowledgment to Susie Long, who was the first person to figure out the true identity of Tom's antagonist. Congratulations.

Jay Heavner

Killing Darkness

Chapter 1

Where am I? How did I get here? He grabbed at the steering wheel in front of him and jerked it to the left, barely avoiding a tree with strands of barbed wire running out of it. The truck bumped around on the narrow county road lacking a centerline or a shoulder. The one headlight working attempted to pierce the darkness around him. Fences hemmed the road in tightly. There was no room for error. He touched the brakes, and the rear tires slipped on the asphalt. After a moment, they grabbed the slick pavement, and the truck slowed to a safer speed, that is, if there were no sharp turns on this country lane. He saw no road signs at all. Where was he?

The second headlight flickered on for a second. A large form stood in the road. *Deer!* He slammed on the brakes. Too late. With a sickening thud, they hit, and the flickering headlight went out. He slid to a halt and backed up to where he'd struck it. After putting the truck in park and seeing no other activity on the road, he grabbed a flashlight lying on the seat and got out. The front of the old pickup had been damaged severely, but it was still drivable. Blood ran and dripped from the point of impact. Coarse brown hair clung to the twisted metal and glass. A large buck with broken legs and other injuries tried to get up, but could not. He walked to a few feet from the maimed animal. To his surprise, he found a handgun in a holster at his side. He pulled the gun out and pointed it at the wounded animal. Its eyes followed his movements. The deer let out a horrible cry, a death-cry. It knew what was coming next.

The abominable bellow shook him to his core, but he knew what he must do. With one shot, he extinguished the animal's life. He looked around into the night blackness but saw nothing. It was still again, too still. He gutted the deer and with great effort, managed to get the bloody carcass into the truck bed. For some reason he could not explain, he left the gate to the truck bed down.

A dim light barely visible shown on what he believed was the horizon. Perhaps soon, with the coming day, he would find out where he was, assuming too, the light was not from a farm on a distant hill.

He drove on. It did seem to be getting brighter. Patches of fog laid at ground level, and a misty cloud hung above the truck. It cut through the fog and made surreal spinning vortexes. The day was getting slightly brighter. Off to the left, he saw many paired points of light. Eyes were staring at him, the accusing alien-like eyes of many goats all looking at him, and they whispered, "Murderer, killer, assassin."

The piercing eyes sent chills through him, but he did know where he was now, the goat farm along Dans Run Road near his home at Short Gap, West Virginia. And he knew where he was going and why.

The dense fog stymied the sun's efforts to illuminate the darkness. He drove on with the goat voices nipping at his ears and crossed a narrow concrete bridge that looked and was nearly a century old. A shiny plaque on it read Ferris Bridge Company, Pittsburgh, Pennsylvania, 1912. The road snaked left and closely paralleled railroad tracks. A bright light appeared, and a piercing train whistle cut the darkness. One hundred cars roared by. The ground shook, and the truck swayed in the turbulence created by the thundering behemoth. His heart pounded in his chest as he drove on. The road pulled away from the tracks and twisted up a hill. Through the fog, a nightlight eerily illuminated an old farmhouse in a cove to the right. The road descended the hill, and the tracks were again by his side, but it was quiet now. He could hear the sound of water rushing over rocks. Yes, he knew where he was. That was the Potomac River, and he was sure he knew where he was going.

The road ascended the hill again. He drove on the serpentine road till it crossed the high ridge, and he took the rutted farm lane to the right. A gate barred his path. He stopped twenty feet away, and it swung in ominously as if it had been expecting him. Terror filled him out as he watched. This was not an automatic gate, and there was nothing visible to explain what he saw. He did not want to go in, but he knew he would continue like a moth heading to the light even knowing he would likely die.

The rising sun and its light gave the area an otherworldly look. He stopped the truck near the old farmhouse. It was here he had nearly been killed, not once, but twice. With his hand, he touched the scar on his head the round from a pistol had made. He should have been shaking, but strange calm permeated him. He got out and walked toward the structure. Something brushed against his ankle, and he jumped back. A calico cat looked up at him and meowed.

He heard a vehicle coming up the farm lane. A large, dark blue, almost black Chevy SUV stopped fifty feet from him. The cat hissed, took off running, and disappeared around the house. The driver shut off the engine and got out. He was of medium to short height and average build. The expensive dark suit he wore was impressive. It contrasted to the old flour sack with two eye holes cut out, which covered his head. He stopped twenty feet from Tom and looked at the bloody deer in the back of the truck, but did not comment on it. The newcomer spoke, "Good morning, Mister Tom Kenney. Somehow, I knew I would find you here this morning. I trust you are well," the electronically altered voice said.

"I believe you're the one who phones me and identifies himself as 'the Benefactor.'"

The sack nodded. "I am he, and you know why I am here."

"You want this to be over. You want the treasure. You want Braddock's lost gold payroll."

The sack nodded again, "Why, you must have read my mind. I trust you have an answer for me."

"I do. I want this to be over too."

"Good. Now we are getting somewhere. What do you have?"

Tom reached under his jacket and pulled out a pistol he pointed at the man known as the Benefactor. "I've got this for you.'

"Tsk, tsk, tsk, and after all, I have done for you. Surely you would not shoot an unarmed man?" He opened his suit jacket slowly to show he carried no weapon.

"This is going to end right, here right now today, and no more games."

"Do you think my death will end it, Mr. Kenney?"

"I believe so. I'll risk it."

"Then do what you must, but remember this. Like a phoenix, I will rise again."

Anger gripped Tom. His face twisted as he took a shooting stance. He braced for recoil and squeezed the trigger time after time until the clip was empty. Round after round had found the body of the Benefactor. Blood flowed from the many wounds, but the Benefactor remained standing.

"Did you think it was that easy to rid yourself of me, Mr. Kenney?"

Tom's mouth stood open in disbelief, and a flame-like one on a candle arose on the sack that covered the head. It quickly spread into a funeral pyre over the whole body that continued to stand. The body turned to grey ash and crumbled, starting at the head. It fell to a heap, and the fire went out entirely. Tom looked at the ashes as a cloud of black smoke began to come from them. It had a sulfur odor that bit as his nostrils. The smoke took the form of a menacing winged bird, and it spoke, "I told you I would rise again. I would be reborn. No mortal can take my life."

It flew into the sky, and as it flew, Tom could hear it speak in an evil way. "You will see me again, Mr. Kenney. I want the treasure you have, and you **will** give it to me."

It became a dot and disappeared. All was still, too still. Tom heard a rustling behind him. He turned around. Standing directly behind him was the monstrous creature. Its eyes looked like flames, and it spoke to Tom. "I am Darkness. Trust me. I will save you."

Tom heard someone wailing, "No, no, nooo!"

He recognized the voice. He was the one screaming like a wild man.

Chapter 2

“No, no, nooo," Tom heard himself cry out. The ground underneath him seemed to be falling away, and he felt himself falling into a deep, dark abyss. "No," he screamed, "Nooo.”

Tom’s body convulsed as he hit bottom. His breath came in gasps. His heart pounded like an Indian war drum as the warriors danced themselves into a frenzy before a coming battle. His eyes began to focus in the near darkness. They darted from side to side. Where was he? His hand touched something, cloth. It covered him from the waist down and was also under him. It was the sheets of his bed in the old farmhouse he called home along Highway Route 28, Short Gap, West Virginia. He was in his own bed. It had all been a dream, a bad dream, one of many he’d had in his life. In years gone by, they’d often been of the horrible battle in the Ia Drang Valley where he had nearly died while a soldier, but lately, they'd been about Braddock’s Gold and real and imagined threats on his life.

He felt around in the bed for his wife, Joann, but she was not there. He let out a sigh of relief. When the PTSD dreams invaded his mind as he slept, he would sometimes react like they were real and strike out at the threat. He’d warned her not to touch him and to get away during these episodes for her safety when these night terrors came. He’d once blackened the eyes of his first wife, Sarah when she’d clenched his arm during one of his nightmares. She never did that again, and Tom was profusely sorry for his defensive reaction. How he loved her. Tragically, she died after being hit head-on by a drunk driver on a local highway.

Tom spoke to the darkness, “Joann, are you there?”

Her quivering voice came from somewhere on the other side of the room. “Yes, I’m here.”

“How bad did I scare you this time?”

“About an eight and a half on the scale of one to ten.”

“Pretty bad, it was then?”

"Yeah, it was. It’s been some time since you became that animated in your sleep.”

“Do you have the baby with you?” he asked.

“She’s over here in her cradle sleeping. She was crying, hungry, and wet, so I took care of her, and I had no more than got her back down when you started to thrash around. I thought it best to see what happened from the safety of the rocking chair over here,” she said.

“I’m glad you did. You know I’m a mess when I get like this. Glad you’re safe.” He stopped. “I believe I told you about how, during a disturbing nightmare like I had tonight, I once punched Sarah between the eyes and blackened them. I thought she was a Viet Cong grabbing me. I felt so bad about that and hoped never to have anything like that happen again. She covered for me by saying she had walked into a door during the night.”

“Yes, you told me several times to make a point, and I never wanted that to happen to me either, so I try to keep my distance when you get like that.”

“You’re a smart lady. Consciously, I’d never want to do that to anyone, especially you, but I know what I’m capable of when the horrors come to me as I sleep.”

"What was your dream about this time? The battle in Vietnam or something else?”

“Something else newer, present time 1998. It concerned the fellow who calls himself the Benefactor.”

“Another one of those, huh?”

"Yeah, it was bizarre. I can remember most of it. It started out with me not knowing where I was, driving an old beater truck and hitting a deer. I shot the wounded animal with a handgun I was packing, gutted it, and threw it in the back of the truck.”

“A true West Virginian, you are Tom. Bringing home your roadkill.”

He smiled. "Yeah, I guess so. Then I drove up to the gate of the old farm where I was nearly killed twice, and the gate opened on its own, drawing me in."

“Like the white whale drew Captain Ahab on.”

"You got it. I pulled up to the old farmhouse, got out, and soon a dark SUV pulled up. The Benefactor got out. He had on a suit, and the cloth sack with two crude eye holes cut out I told you about was on his head. I told him I wanted this to be over. He said he did too.”

Tom was silent.

“Don’t keep me in suspense, Tom. And then what happened?”

“I shot him.”

“You shot him?” she said, surprised.

"Yeah, I shot him, over and over again, round after round from my handgun. Six or seven times. Blood poured out of the wounds, but he just stood there like nothing happened.”

“That’s very scary.”

"Tell me about it, and it gets better. He told me I couldn’t kill him. His body caught fire and then crumbled into ashes. Smoke came from them, and it formed a winged beast like a phoenix and flew away laughing hideous like at me. It disappeared, and the next thing I knew, it was behind me. I turned, and it spoke to me. I think it said, ‘I am the Darkness. I will save you.' That’s when I woke up screaming. It took a few moments to figure out where I was and realize it was just another bad dream.”

“That’s really weird. Any idea what it meant?”

"No, maybe it'll make more sense in the morning, but right now, it's just another horrible dream." He stopped. “And I can’t believe the baby slept right through all this.”

“She did,” Joann said. “Little Brook was dead to the world and sawing logs during your unpleasantness.”

Tom said, “My dad would tell me how when I was that size, and he built this house from the basement up, my baby bed would be in the same room, and I could sleep right through all the activity, all the saws going and hammers pounding."

“Well, Brook does have half your genes, so I guess it would be natural she reacted in some of the same ways.”

"Yeah, I guess so. She’s our little blessing, alright. The doctors said you would never carry her full term. Even if she was born a few months early, it’s still a miracle she made it.”

“There were lots of people praying for us as you well know, Tom. Never forget that.”

"Yeah, besides your earthy doctor, you had a heavenly Physician who deals in miracles.”

"How right you are on that. Doctor Brown said as much. He's a super doctor when it comes to prenatal, but pretty hardcore when it comes to his feelings about God, religion, or the supernatural. I knew his reputation on this and almost went elsewhere because of it. Just the same, I knew I could not have gotten better care anywhere than from Doctor Brown.”

“You’re correct on that. I was satisfied very much with his care. He bent over backward to see you had the best available. I think your faith and example affected old Mister Hardshell.”

“He told me as much one day when he stopped in to visit my room at the hospital.”

“I think our little wonder affected everyone at the hospital. We had more than our share of nurses and doctors stopping in. The whole wing of the hospital was buzzing like a beehive because of our little girl. Oh, and one more thing while I’m thinking about it. Padre called and wants to meet you for breakfast at Linda’s tomorrow morning. I told him yes. Hope I did right. I knew you hadn’t heard from him in ages and would jump at the chance to talk. Was I right or not?”

“You done the right thing. I'd have canceled a meeting with the president to hear what he’s been up to and why he hasn’t called. It has to be important. I’m glad you said yes for me.”

“Thanks. Glad we were on the same page.”

“Hey,” Tom said. “Why are you still in that chair? Why aren’t you over here in bed with me? And I’m lonely.” Tom stuck his lower lip out for effect.

“I can hear and see that even in this blackness,” said Joann. “Are you sure it’s safe for me now?”

“I think the bad dreams are gone. Very unlikely they’ll come again tonight, but is it safe for you in this bed? You never know what kind of hairy animal you might find there.” In the darkness, Joann could hear the suggestive tone to his voice.

“Well,” she said with a slight purr. “I’ll just have to take my chances." With that said, she crossed the room, sliding across the bed into Tom's waiting arms and cuddled up to his warm bare chest.

“Much better. Nothing like having the mother of your child snuggled up next to you.”

She squeezed him a little closer. They were quiet as they enjoyed the moment. She turned her head and asked, “Tom, do you still think we made the right decision, you know, no more children?”

Tom sighed. “Yes, I believe we did. God gave us one miracle. The doctors said it was unbelievable you were able to carry Brook as long as you did. I don’t think I could go through this again. They all said if you got pregnant again, it would likely not end well, for the baby, or you. As much as I know you love children, I think it’s best for us.”

She nodded. "I know. My head says one thing, and my heart says another. Life sure can be complicated."

“Miriah did get her wish for a little sister.”

“That’s true. She’s not even complaining about changing her sister’s stinky diapers. It’s gonna be all right. We’ll get through this with God’s help.”

"You know Jo; every child is a miracle. When you think of how the itty-bitty sperm and egg get together and have all the information in that little bundle to make a baby human child, I don't understand how anyone could not believe in miracles and the supernatural. It just couldn't happen by sheer chance and dumb luck. Someone designed all of this."

“True, so very true.”

They were quiet for some time. They got closer and kissed.

Tom said, “Are you thinking what I’m thinking?”

A little growl escaped from her throat. “I believe so, big boy. No sleep for the lion tonight.”

“Oooh,” slipped from his lips. “Just the same sweetie, some good lovin’ should help this ole lion sleep better for the rest of the night.”

"Hope I can. Between your snoring and episodes and the baby needing attention, my recent periods of sleep have been somewhat less than pleasant dreams. It never ceases to amaze me how a mother can hear the slightest whimper from her child, but a man can sleep through it all totally oblivious even if a hurricane was to spring up in the bedroom.”

Tom said, "Yeah, I've noticed that too. Sarah said something similar when our boys were young. Now, enough talk. Isn’t it time we get down to some serious lovin’?”

“You know,” she purred, “in the wild, a lion can have sex sixty times a day.”

“Don’t expect that from this old fellow. I can hold my own, but not that often. You do know there is a downside for the little lioness?”

“And that is?”

"Lion's sex only lasts less than a minute each time, and we humans can go on much more than that.”

“I knew there had to be a downside for the King of the Beasts. Glad I got you and not ole Leo.”

With a quick move, the couple slipped out of their nightwear, slid together, and began to kiss and hug passionately. Joann pulled her lips away from Tom’s and said, “Well, Mister King, the lioness is more than ready. What’s taking you so long?”

Tom smiled, “Well, you know what they say. Once a king, always a king….”

She chimed in with him, “But once a knight’s enough.”

They kissed again. Nothing more needed to be said. The fun had begun.

Chapter 3

The old man stirred in his sleep. He opened one blurry eye and surveyed the darkness. The place looked somewhat familiar. He'd done it again-fallen asleep on the couch in the great room at his retreat everyone called the Fortress because it was. The clock on the wall read 3:00. He pulled the cover away. His hand searched around for the bottle of Jack Daniels he knew he had not finished off. It had to be here somewhere, but it wasn't.

Jairo. Jairo had put the cover on him and picked the bottle up. The old man knew, and there was no point in looking further for it. Jairo would have poured anything remaining down the drain. He felt angry for a moment. How he could have used another stiff drink to numb himself, but how could he stay mad with Jairo, the man who had been with him for years and been nothing but loyal? Jairo always dumped any remaining alcohol out. It was a small price to pay for the complete faith he had in Jairo and Rosa. He'd just do what he always did, pick up another bottle today when he was out. The old man remembered the first time he had seen Jairo and Rosa, his wife, that summer in 1979 nearly twenty years ago. They both spoke some English, mostly broken, but he was able to learn that Jairo had been in the Somoza government that had recently fallen to the Sandinistas in Nicaragua, and she was a nurse. They had escaped with the clothes on their backs and little more. Someone in the

Central American county had given them a contact name in the United States, and through a convoluted route, they had reached him.

The old man needed someone to help at the Fortress. His various sources had checked their stories out, and they were who they said they were. They were also here illegally. The old man's young daughter was dying from Lupus, and his wife was consumed with fear and depression from worrying about her. He explained his needs to them, and Jairo and Rosa agreed to work for him. He would see they provided for and safe from authorities, and they would care for his family and the compound. He warned them he would not tolerate disloyalty and let them know it was very unwise to disappoint him. They had understood the veiled threat and never done anything contrary to his wishes in the decades since. The trust had become mutual, and now the old man would trust the two with his life.

He swung his feet over the side and sat up. His hair was in his face, and he pushed it back with his hand, and he had to pee. The old man nearly fell as he got up. The alcohol content in his body was still high. He stumbled to the bathroom, relieved himself, and found his way back to his couch though he nearly went down when he slipped on a throw rug. He noted the view screen on the monitor had gone black and turned itself off.

What was Tom Kenney doing tonight? He hoped he was sleeping well, and Tom's PTSD would clear up enough to allow him to remember where the gold payroll of General Braddock was buried. The old man was patient, but he hoped this would soon be over. He was tempted to turn the equipment on and use the infrared spy mode, which also had thermal detection. It had come in handy recently when he showed the Congressman the video of him and his secretary in a heated moment and a compromising position. The Congressman had readily agreed not to block a revenue bill the old man wanted. Buried in it was money for a government front office that saw he received funding for more advanced spying and surveillance equipment. No, he would not do that to Tom. Spying and information collecting was one thing. Voyeurism was another. Let him have his privacy. He had come to like Tom from his clandestine phone calls with him and when he had talked with Tom face to face, though Tom was none the wiser of who he really was. He hoped Tom had pleasant dreams. Maybe he himself could get back to sleep. He hoped that was the case. He rested his head on the pillow and pulled the cover over himself. Soon he was fast asleep and snoring.

Two figures approached the sleeping man through the darkness and stopped near him.

"Is he asleep?"

"He sleeps like a baby, el bebé."

"Good. We can do what we need to, and he will never know."

They took a step closer and raised their hands high toward the unconscious man.

The man whispered, "Dios, You know what manner of man this is before us. Some parts bueno, some parts malo, but no one is beyond Your reach, Your eyes, or Your gracia. Open his corazón, his heart to the truth. He needs You more than he can even imaginar. Protect him from those that would seek to harm him. Amén."

"Amén." They were both quiet for a moment before the woman spoke. "Jairo, do you think he will ever change for the good?"

"We can only pray, Rosa. We can only pray for him. May he have pleasant dreams tonight."

"Si, Papa. We need to get some sleep. Morning, de mañana, is coming soon pronto, and we have mucho to do."

"Si, Mama. Pray his dreams are fresco, sweet like new wine."

The couple crept off to their bedroom in the large compound and were soon asleep. Little could they realize their prayers for cleansing dreams for the old man would be granted this very night. Other prayers were to be answered in Dios's own perfect timing.

Chapter 4

1943

"Gino. Get the hell in here," shouted his father. "I want you now!"

The time had come. Today was the day. Today the beating would stop, or someone would die. Sixteen-year-old Little Gino took a deep breath, let it out, and walked around the corner and through the door. He inhaled in an involuntary gasp when he saw the blood on his mother's face and dress. She had blood on the hands that covered her eyes, and she'd crawled up against the wall. Her legs were pulled up to her body, and she was crying out in sobs, "Please stop, please stop."

"I'll stop when I'm damn well ready," Big Gino said. He drew his fist back.

"You will stop right now," Little Gino said with all the determination he could find in him.

"You? You think you of all people can stop me? Little you?"

"You will stop, or I will kill you. You will not ever hit my mother again."

"You think a runt like you can stop me?" He took a step toward his son.

"You will stop right there. I brought some help." He pulled out the .38 caliber Police Special revolver.

Big Gino's eyes widened ever so slightly. "How did you get that? Give it to me if you know what's good for you, pipsqueak. Give it to me." He took a step forward, and Little Gino pulled the trigger.

A curse roared from Big Gino. He put his hand on the bloody tip of his ear. "You almost missed me, punk."

Little Gino's face was hard. "I hit what I was aiming at. If I wanted you dead, you would be now. Stop beating my mother or else."

"Or else what? You got lucky. You think you got the guts to kill your old man?" He took another step forward, and Little Gino pulled the trigger again.

Big Gino cursed again and put his hand to the bloody tip of his other ear. His eyes revealed the truth that if not for the expert shooting of his son, he would be dead. "Where'd you learn to shoot like that? You could have killed me."

"At the range. They said I was a natural. The round just goes where I want it to."

"At the range?" Big Gino repeated. "About time you found something you could do right."

The insult hurt Little Gino, but he was determined to mask his feeling and control the rage inside of him. "If you ever, ever hurt my mother again, I will kill you."

Big Gino nodded his head, bloody ears and all. “I believe you would. You may have some potential, after all.” He stepped back and walked out of the room using the door on the other side of the big room.

Little Gino looked at his mother curled up in the fetal position. He put the gun safety on, bent down, and put his arm around her to comfort her. “He will never harm you again, or I will kill him.”

“No, Gino, no. You mustn’t kill your father. He’s been angry like that since your brother died in the war. It’s not his fault he’s like that. You mustn’t.”

“I will not if he leaves you alone, but if he does not, nothing will stop me. I mean it.”

“You sound like him, Gino, when someone has crossed him. You know what he’s capable of. Don’t be like him.”

"I will do what I think is right. I will do what I need to do. Now let me help you into the bathroom, and you can clean up yourself."

“Okay.”

He helped her to her feet and gently took her to the nearby bathroom. “You be okay?” he asked.

"Yes, I'll be okay with a son like you." She weakly smiled at him, and he returned her smile. He pulled the door closed and went back to the big room to wait. When he walked in, he found his father slumped in an overstuffed chair, a band-aid on each ear, a half-drunk fifth of whiskey between his legs, and the ever-present cigarette in his hand. He looked at his son and asked, “You really would have killed me, wouldn’t you?”

Little Gino smiled cruelly.

"Yeah, you would. You really would. I didn't think you had what it takes, but I guess I misjudged you. You may just have what it takes to run the organization. Your brother was to do that, but that was before this damned war happened, and he got himself killed. You think you got what it takes to run a syndicate like the family?"

"If you behave yourself and leave my mother alone and I do not have to kill you, yes, I believe I could learn what I have to, to take over."

A hard smile came to half of Big Gino's face. "Yeah, you may have what it takes. You want to shake on it?"

"No, I do not trust you right now. This may only be a ruse to get close and teach me a lesson."

"Well done, young man. Well done. You may make it, after all."

Little Gino's cruel smile grew. "And if I get that close right now, I do not trust myself not to change my mind and kill you."

The smile left his father's face. He put his hand to his chin and rubbed it. Then he coughed a cough that continued to grow ever worse. Big Gino cleared his throat loudly. His eyes met his son's. His voice was hoarse as he said, "Yeah, I think I've underestimated you. I think you may very well make it." He paused. "It's a deal. No more hurting your mom, and I teach you the business. Sounds good to me."

Little Gino said nothing for a moment. He thought about what his father had said and also about the harsh, throaty rasping of his voice. It started some months before and was getting worse. A small grin came to his face. He said, "Sounds good to me, too, but I may still one day decide to shoot you just the same."

"Yeah, I think you'll make it. This could be the beginning of a great friendship." He coughed again. "Damn cigarettes. Probably kill me if one of my rivals don't first."

Little Gino nodded. For once, he agreed with everything his father said. Time would tell how they both played out.

Chapter 5

The Next Day

Gino sat at the table in the middle of the lunchroom with his back to the wall. From here, he could see everything that was going on. No one would sneak up on him at this spot. For the most part, most of the students left him alone. No one was sitting in any of the chairs near him. Few wanted to associate with the boy they thought was a Mafia Don's son. No, his worries were on the few other boys that would attack him, because, like him, they were mobster's sons. He'd had his run-ins with them before, but he was looking forward to the next time. His self-defense class training would be a big surprise for them. It would be his turn to turn the tables on his tormentors. He hoped a good thrashing of them would turn the tide, and then they would leave him alone.

From a side door, he saw a boy a year older than him enter the room. He scanned the room, and when his eyes saw Gino, he quickly made a beeline for him. "How's it going, Gino?"

"It's going better than can be expected. And you, Michael?"

"Pretty good, except Sister Mary Ellaphant got on my case again. Old battle-ax. I tell you, I think she's sexually frustrated, she is."

“Nuns get none,” Gino said.

"Yeah, guess that's where the name comes from."

They laughed at that.

“Sister Mary Ellaphant. She’s so fat it’d take ten men to hug her,” Michael said.

“No hearse for her when she dies. It will take a Mack truck to lug her to the cemetery.”

“Ain’t that the truth. So Gino, what’s new with you?”

“I had it out with my old man yesterday. He hit my mother again.”

Michael's eyes widened, and a whistle escaped his lips. "Wow, and you're still standing. I don't see no black eyes or bruising. What happened?"

"He hit her, and I got the gun, the long-barreled police special. I told him I would shoot him if he hit her again. He came after me, and I shot the tip of his ear off. He screamed and cursed. Told me it was a lucky shot and a bad one if I meant to kill him. I told him the bullet went where I wanted it to go. He did not believe me and came at me again. I shot the tip off his other ear, and he believed me."

“I told you; you’re a natural. It’s like you had been born with a gun in your hand.”

“So it seems. And then he did the unexpected. He said he thought he had underestimated me. He asked me if I thought I would be interested in learning to take over the family business.”

“Yowzer. Now that is something. He wants you to run it? What did you say?”

"I said I was willing. I also told him I would kill him if he ever hit my mother again."

"Bet that got his attention."

"It did. I saw his eyes widen though he tried to suppress it. And then he smiled and said, 'I'll bet you would too."

"Wow."

"If I read him right, his expression said several things. One, I would really kill my own father if he hurt my mother again. Two, he was surprised I had it in me to kill. And three, maybe he had found someone to take over for him. I had overheard him talking with my older brother about him being the heir to the family business and taking over after the war was over. His getting killed in France ended his life and that dream. I think my father takes some of that anger out on my mother. He better find another outlet if he wants to live."

"Why would you want to stay in a business like yours? You could get out and go legit. Others have done it."

"I know, but I remember him telling Billy if a strong leader did not take over and establish himself as the boss quickly, a war would break out among the families in the organization, and many people would die, a lot of them innocent bystanders who would get pulled in or caught in the crossfire. It seems a better alternative, anyway. You know, keep it in the family."

"I guess so. You have to do what you think is right. Me, I want to join the military and kill Nazis. I keep hearing what they are doing to Jews over there. Ain't right. They need to be stopped, and that means blood must be spilled, their blood."

Gino smiled. Michael Levi was the only Jewish kid at the Catholic school, so it was no surprise why these two shunned kids became companions. "Say," Gino said. "Do you think they have a place for a guy that's a natural-born good shot in the military?'

"I'm sure they do. With the way you shoot, they will send you to sniper school. I heard they need a whole bunch of those. We can kill Nazis together, and the war will be over in no time."

"I like that idea. Hey, let us freak them out. Want to do what we did that one time?"

"Yes, and Sister Mary Ellaphant just came into the room. She'll blow a head gasket, but it will be worth it."

"Okay, then. Let us do it."

Gino walked around the table with a determined look on his face. Michael squared off against him, and slowly the room went silent.

When it was so quiet you could hear a pin drop, the two boys ran at each other and hit chest to chest. They bounced back from each other and yelled, "Oorah!" and then hit again and yelled, "Oorah!" again.

"You boys, stop that!" screamed Sister Mary Ella.

"Yes, ma'am," they mocked.

"You two, you have detention today and tomorrow."

"Yes, ma'am," they said again, less mocking this time.

Sister Mary Ella's face was red, and she looked like steam would soon be coming out of her ears.

Michael said to Gino, "Let's shake and sit down."

“Good idea. It will get us out of the bullseye and let her save face.”

They did that and sat down. Slowly the others in the room turned back to what they had been doing, and a noisy din returned to the room.

“So, detention for two days,” Michael said.

“But it was worth it. Did you see the look on her face? She looked like she was going to blow like a volcano.”

Michael grinned wickedly. "Yeah, let's do it again sometime soon.”

“I like that idea. And while we are in detention, I can show you a few more self-defense moves and a couple of offensive ones, too.”

“You do that and tell me more about how you are going to kill Nazis in the military.”

"I will do that, and I have some other ideas too you might like.”

“Such as?”

“It will have to wait until detention.”

“This should be good.”

Gino nodded. "It is, and you will be surprised.”

Chapter 6

Christmas Eve 1946

Little Gino sat in a private booth off to the side of the central area of Luigi's Restaurant. The family, his family, owned it. It provided a place where the upper crust of Baltimore could let down their hair, and the business of the city could be hashed out away from public scrutiny. Deals were made as pockets were discretely lined with money, payouts, and paybacks. He waited for his friend, who would soon arrive. How much had he changed? He would soon know. It was 4 PM, and the restaurant would officially close at 6.

Little Gino sipped on his National Bohemian Beer. Mr. Boh, the mustached, one-eyed mascot, stared back at him from the can of "Natty Boh" as it was known locally. He never could figure out why Mr. Boh only had one eye, but he knew the answer that was always given, "Gunther's got it." That was the motto of another beer maker, Gunther Brewing Company, located in Baltimore.

He heard the bell on the front door ring. Someone had come in. He looked at the mirror and saw a slim man wearing a long military-style coat. The collar was pulled up around his neck to protect him from the cold wind blowing off the harbor, or did he have another reason to hide his features? The man spoke to Maria, who was the head cashier. She was one tough cookie who could hold her own against most men, and a .45 discretely located below the cash register on a shelf could take care of any problems. Little Gino knew she knew how to use it. He relaxed as the man put the collar down as he asked Maria something. She looked to the room where Little Gino was seated. “Hey Gino, the man here says he knows you, and you're expecting him.”

“Send him back, Maria,” he yelled back.

She pointed to the room, and the man walked between the tables, turned left, and entered the private room. He smiled, "Hello, Gino. It's been a long time."

Gino lifted his eyes to the other man's eyes. It had that thousand-yard stare of a man who had seen too much combat. “Hello, Michael, my friend. It’s been too long. Have a seat. Want a brew?”

“Sound great.”

“Maria, have Ginger get us two Natty Bohs.”

“Sure thing, LG. Coming right up.”

“LG?” Michael asked. “Is that you?”

"Yes. Little Gino grew up, and so they changed it. My father is now BG, Big Gino."

"Yeah, that makes sense."

"Want some food? We have the best spaghetti with meatballs in all of Baltimore."

Michael shook his head. “Thanks, but no thanks. Still haven’t got my appetite back. The war, you know.”

“Yes, I know. Some of the things I saw I wish I could forget.”

Michael dropped his eyes to the table and said nothing.

From around the corner came a waitress carrying a tray with four beers on it. She set it down on the table, smiled, and left without saying anything.

Little Gino spoke as she left, “Thanks, Ginger. We won’t be ordering food.”

She turned her head around, smiled slightly, and left.

When she was out of hearing range, Michael said, “She don’t say much, does she?”

“No, only what’s necessary and less, and she makes a point to hear even less. Just the food and drink orders and none of the business conversations, you know what I mean?”

"Yeah, I know what you mean. How's your father doing?"

"Poorly. He has throat cancer, and he can only talk using a talkbox, a Sonovox, since the surgery. It is spreading, and he is dying."

“War or peace, seems death never takes a holiday. What did you do during the war? You did go?”

“Yes, I did. I enlisted when I turned eighteen. Father said nothing, and Mother cried her heart out. The thought of losing both of her sons nearly drove her crazy.”

“I see. Did you make it over there before it ended?”

"I did. And you were right about my shooting skills. The Army sent me to sniper school, and I had the best scores they had ever recorded. They ran me through the class at super speed, and I found myself in Germany closing in on the Fuhrer and company in the last days of the war. First, I had a crash course with another sniper who showed me the essentials on how not to get killed, especially from a German sniper whose job was to kill me first and any other Allied forces he could. I must have learned very well as my mentor was killed by one of them, and I killed the Jerry sniper and many more Krauts before the surrender." He stopped. "That's my story. Were you successful in killing all those Nazis you wanted to?"

That far off thousand-yard stare came back to his eyes. He was silent for a moment. "Yes, I did. I fought, and I fought, and I fought for days without sleep or rest. I saw things no human should see in a thousand years, such carnage and destruction. I was there when they liberated the concentration camps. I saw hundreds of emaciated, rotting bodies shoved into mass graves with bulldozers. I can still see the glazed-over eyes of corpses and smell the decaying bodies." He put his head down and lowered his eyes to the table. "You're the first person I've been able to tell this to."

They said nothing for a few moments and drank the first beer in silence. LG spoke, "If you ever need to talk brother, I will be there."

"Thanks. I appreciate it. People ask about the war, treat me like some kind of a hero. I know the Nazis had to be defeated, but there are times I feel dead inside. People who have never been there have no idea of what war is like. There's no way to explain so I say, 'Thank God it's over.'"

"Yes, thank God it is over. May it never happen again." He raised his Natty Boh in a toast, and Michael clanged his can again Little Gino's. The two took big swigs and set the cans down. "How's your mother, Michael?"

Michael's face drained. "She's dying. That is why the Army gave me leave time. She does not have long and… I need to tell you this. She's not really my mom, but my sister. It was easier to get us

Jews out of Germany that way." There was a moment of silence. "I have to arrange for her funeral and decide what is to become of little Mike, remember him?"

"Yes, your brother, who was really your nephew. He should be about six now."

"That's the one. I don't know what I'm gonna do. I wanted to stay in the Army, help clean up the mess from the war, and maybe even make a career of the military."

Little Gino thought for a moment. "I may have a solution concerning your nephew. I know a family in the Family that is childless and has always wanted a son. I can vouch for them."

"Thanks, I keep that in mind. I don't have options. And how's your family, you know the one I'm talking about. You once told me all hell would break loose in Baltimore if a strong boss did not appear, and a smooth transaction to a new don didn't happen."

"I trust you like a brother, Michael. I am the new boss of all the families. When my father got too sick to attend the meetings, we wired his talkbox at his spot at the table so he could still run the show."

"How did that go over?"

"As you guessed, like a lead balloon. Two of the underbosses walked out, and as luck would have it, were run over by a city bus on the sidewalk in front of here. What a mess that was cleaning up."

"Just their dumb bad luck."

"So it would seem. Two other dissenters died under unusual circumstances. One shot himself while cleaning his gun, and the other was killed by a stray bullet that came from somewhere, perhaps a hunter. With these men dead, a war was averted. Lives were spared. We have peace. I am now the voice from the box they hear."

"So, it would seem." He paused, "So I'm talking to the new boss. I know things will go well with you in charge."

"Michael Levy, if you ever need work, I know I could find something for you to do. Consider that and what I said about your brother, I mean, nephew."

"I will. Is your father really dying? I mean, he was always such a tough, strong man."

"Like your sister, his remaining days are few. The pain eats him up. Morphine is the only thing that gives him relief, and the doses must be bigger and bigger as time goes on. If cancer does not kill him soon, the morphine will. Nurses are always in the house nearby when needed. He talks crazy sometimes, to imaginary people he sees and about a nutty tale about a lost gold payroll for some long-dead General, General Braddock. It seems members of my family have been looking for it since before the American Revolution. Back then, the family's name was the French Geoffrey. It was Anglicized when they came east and settled in Catholic Baltimore."

"Braddock's Gold. Yeah, I heard of it. Father Murphy, who taught history at the church school, was a real local history buff, and I remember him talking about it. He made it sound like it was a fortune waiting to be found."

"My father seems to think so too. It is hard to tell what is true and what is the morphine talking. I shall look into this after his passing. He babbles on about the family history. He says many of them looked, but some of my ancestors were obsessed with finding it and never did."

Michael finished off the last of his second beer and set the can down. He looked at his watch. “My, how time flies. I need to get going, but it’s funny how with you it seems like it was just yesterday we talked.”

"With true friends, you can trust that is the way it is. Consider my offers and get back with me when you decide what you must do. And remember what I said, I can find a job for you if you ever need it and want it."

"I will. Give my best to your father."

“Likewise, for your sister. I will pray and light a candle for her.”

“Thank you. I must go. Till we meet again.”

With that, Michael rose from the chair and quickly exited the restaurant. Little Gino sat at the table and sipped the last of his beer. He had made his choice in his life's direction. He was the new acting boss of bosses, and soon his father would pass. Decisions would have to be made. He wanted to keep the peace, expand his power, and more. The sky would be the limit. No, there would be no limit. He could reign supreme like Solomon, have everything he wanted, maybe even find and solve the legend of Braddock’s Gold. And the Olympics were scheduled to start again in 1948 in London. With his shooting skills, maybe he could find gold there too.

Chapter 7

The Next Morning, 1998

It was just a short drive, a mile or so, to Linda's Restaurant, but Tom had much to think about. Father Frank was the priest of the local Catholic church and lovingly known as Padre or the Padre. He was also Tom's closest friend in the world after his family. Padre had been strangely silent and not contacted Tom in a large number of months. He had sent a gift certificate for diapers from Martin's grocery store and a card, but all he had done was sign his name to it without comment other than the usual congratulations on the birth of the baby. Tom knew a lot was going on in Padre's life. He had wanted to contact his friend during this silent time, but something in his spirit told him not to. It was better for Padre to work his problems out himself and wait for him to contact Tom. Now he had, and Tom had many questions he would like answered. As a pastor, Tom considered the information the Padre had given confidential and had not even shared it even with Joann though she could tell something was up and not right. Being married to a man who had to keep secrets from his wife was not always easy, and she was a curious woman.

What was going through Padre's mind? Why hadn't he called? What decisions had he made, if any? What of his girlfriend in Pittsburgh? How was she after the miscarriage of their unplanned child?

What of his conflict about being a celibate priest and their desire to marry? What had he, or she, or they, decided to do? Tom had so many questions. He felt like he was going to explode from anticipation. He wanted answers, but would they be forthcoming? Tom let out a heavy sigh as he rounded another of the numerous curves of snaking WV Route 28. Something caught his eye in the tall weeds and brush down over the bank. It moved swiftly up the road bank and stood in his lane. DEER! The glare from its eyes pierced his and found its way to his very soul. "Murderer, killer, assassin," they said.

Tom slammed on the brakes and left forty feet of rubber as he slid in the old Chevy pickup toward the stationary deer. At the last moment, the phantom seemed to leap away and was gone. Tom's heart pounded wildly in his chest. He let off the brake pedal and proceeded on. It was too real to be a hallucination, or was it? His hands trembled on the steering wheel. A sharp turn ahead now had his attention. He was on the narrow shoulder before he could recover. The truck fishtailed as the rear broke loose. It threw gravel vehemently. A dust cloud formed and spun turning wildly and upon itself. With great effort, Tom brought the truck under control. His heart felt like it was going to jump out of his body. Trembling, he drove the last half mile, turned right onto Old Furnace Road, and then a quick left into the parking lot at the restaurant. He sat his vehicle as he tried to regain his composure. Now he had more questions than before.

Tom looked around the parking lot for familiar vehicles. He saw Mr. Whitacre's Chevy Impala parked in front. It looked like his wife still had him on his diet the doctor recommended, and it looked like he was going around it by stopping at Linda's to fill his ample tummy. One day over a cup of coffee, the old man had confessed food was one of his few real joys in life now that his love life had gone to pot because of his condition. Tom had almost blurted out that he believed the old man's love life would return if he only lost the extra weight. The wife would find him more attractive, and his condition should improve when the extra girth was gone, but he wisely caught himself at the last moment and merely nodded his head.

He saw some construction trucks of local builders, Knotts Brothers, and also Dowden Construction Company. Parked side-by-side was a brown UPS truck and a white FedEx truck. A Caporales' Bakery truck sat close to the highway. Now he knew why the bread at Linda's tasted so good. Tom sat for another minute and felt better. He climbed out of the truck and made his way to the door. When he walked in, all eyes turned to see who the newcomer was. The UPS driver sat next to the FedEx man at the bar, and they went back to their conversion. Mr. Whitacre had a guilty look on his face, but Tom smiled at him and walked to the far corner where Father Frank was seated. It was obvious why he had chosen that spot. It was the most private spot available in the large open room. As Tom neared the table in the far corner, big black Father Frank rose and greeted Tom with a bear hug that nearly crushed the breath out of the smaller man. In his booming voice that drew everyone's attention, the Padre said, “Hello, my brother from another mother. It’s so good to see you again.”

When the air came back into Tom, he said, “We may have had different mothers, but we both have the same Father.”

“Amen to that,” roared Padre. “Have a seat. That coffee you love so much is coming, and seeing as I know you like a brother, I took the liberty of ordering for you, a number 5, biscuits with sausage gravy, home fries, and a side of kosher bacon.”

Tom sat down and noticed that every eye that had been watching them was now going back to whatever it was they were doing before the Padre's boisterous greeting. “That sounds very good to me, but where, oh where, did you find kosher bacon?”

"Well, I may have done a little stretchin’ of the truth on that one. I think the Lord will forgive me for doing so. He's forgiven so much more.”

Tom could tell there would be more coming when the Padre was ready to continue. "So how you been, old buddy? It's been a long time, and I was beginning to worry about you. I figured you'd call when you were ready."

At that time, Deb appeared with a cup in one hand and a coffee pot in the other. She poured Tom a cup and freshened up Father Frank's cup. She said, "Your food should be coming up soon. I saw Lois cooking it just a moment ago."

“That sounds super to me, Deb,” the Padre said. “I don't get in here enough, and the food's great, and the atmosphere's always welcoming.”

“Thanks for the compliments, Father,” she said. “You know you're a stranger here only once.”

Father Frank nodded, “Yes, I do. I've been in some places where I was merely tolerated, but never made to feel welcome.”

Deb smiled, “We treat everyone the same here. We see only one color, green.”

The three laughed at the little joke.

“Hey, Deb. Can I get a warmer up?” came a voice from several tables over.

“Sure thing Jim,” she replied to him. “Sorry guys, I would love to chit-chat, but duty calls.”

“Gotcha,” Padre said.

“Your meals should be out real soon. Trust me on that one.” She turned and walked over to Jim, who was waving his coffee cup. Tom noticed a slight eye roll from Deb, who gave the waiting man a plastic forced smile as she walked over and filled his cup.

“I know why you like coffee so well, Tom,” Padre said.

His curiosity aroused, he asked, “Okay, I’ll bite. Why do I like coffee so well?”

“Because coffee stands for Christ Offers Forgiveness For Everyone Everywhere.”

Tom smiled, “Hey, I like that. I’ll have to remember that. Christ Offers Forgiveness For Everyone Everywhere. Very catchy.”

Tom looked at his friend across the table and said, “It's been a long time since I've heard from you. I know you must have had a good reason for the wait. What is it you wanted to talk to me about? What do you need to tell me?”

The Padre let out a long breath and began to speak in little more than a whisper. No one sitting a booth away would be able to hear what he had to say. "I've got a lot to tell you, and I didn't want to contact you till I had it all figured out."

“I'm all ears.”

"I suppose you're wondering about my girlfriend and me in Pittsburgh. This may take a little while. After we grieved for our child she miscarried, we both felt we needed some time to think. We didn't see or call each other for a month. I couldn't stand it any longer and called her. We got together and had a long talk. We decided we would start anew and this time, no sex. We both wanted to make sure our physical desires weren't clouding our better judgment. We were doing at least one thing right now. After about three months, we started talking about marriage. We both wanted to tie the knot, but you know this priest thing of mine got in the way. I should have been born a thousand years ago when it was okay before that one old pope had his revelation and stopped priestly marriage. Tom, you know that this imperfect man loves the Lord. He's the only perfect One, and He gave us His instruction book called the Bible for life here on earth. No man, but Him is free from error and in my humble opinion that includes the pope. I wish I could marry and still be a priest, but that's not an option, so I've decided to turn in my resignation very shortly."

"But what will you do? I know you love what you are doing."

"I do, but my mind has been made up. I've crossed my own private Rubicon. The city of Pittsburgh has been looking for police officers, especially men and women of my race. I was an MP in the military, so I already know a lot about law enforcement training. They still want me to take a bunch of classes, including the infamous Hell Week, to prove to them what I'm made of. I know it's not going to be easy, but it's what I think He wants me to do. Also, my training as a priest will get me in as a chaplain, and there's a lot of cops and their families that need spiritual instruction and support. Cops deal daily with issues the average family never has to. Those men and women in blue never know if they'll be coming home at the end of a shift. All it takes is one dirtbag or nutcase to end their lives.

"And one last thing, I grew up in the slums of Baltimore. A lot of the kids who I knew there are either in jail, wasting their lives away on drugs and alcohol, or dead. I might just be that guiding force that can save a few in the poorer sections of Pittsburgh. My dad took off when me and my twin brother were young, but my mom's brothers were always there when mom needed a hand with us. Pardon my French, but I got my ass kicked numerous times by them when I got too big for my britches. And I deserved every one of them, probably more. They weren't perfect men, but they could put the fear of the Lord in you.

"My uncles loved baseball. I remember when they somehow got tickets for a game in Washington. They loaded me and Freddie up in the back of their old station wagon with a cooler full of beer between us. Whenever they finished a beer, a Natty Boh, our job was to pass them a fresh one from the cooler. They drank one after another on the way down and on the way back. Somehow the cops never bothered us, and somehow we made it through in one piece."

"Just one question. What's a Natty Boh?"

"It was the beer of Baltimore, National Bohemian. You can still find it. Not sure who owns it now. The company's been sold several times."

"So how soon before the wedding? It sounds like you've got it all planned out."

"Some, but not all of it. We want to get married soon, in a couple of months, and we're looking for a preacher." A big grin appeared on the Padre's dark face. "My friend, any chance would you be available? The bride-to-be has never met you, but after she heard my glowing description of you, we both agreed that you were the one we wanted for the job. Please?"

"Padre, I'd be honored to do it. We'll have to find a convenient date for both of us."

At that time, Deb showed up with their food and placed it in front of them. "Here you go, fellows. It took a little longer than I thought it would."

"Did it?" Tom said. "We were so busy talking. We lost all talk of time."

“And they say women are bad,” smirked Deb.

“They are,” Padre said.

Deb’s smirk on her face got bigger. “Now, you two, don't get sassy with me.”

“Not us,” Tom said. “We wouldn't think of it.”

“Hey Deb, I need some more coffee,” came a familiar voice.

They turned to see Jim waving his cup. Deb turned back to the fellows and rolled her eyes. "Looks like Mr. Bottomless Pit needs more coffee. I wouldn't mind it so much if he was a decent tipper, which he's not. I'll take care of him and see you two get more coffee. Fair enough?”

They gave her two thumbs up, and she left.

“Now,” Padre said. “I've told you what's been happening in my life. What's been happening with you? Anything exciting you want to tell me about?”

Chapter 8

Tom let out a deep breath. "Well, as Charles Dickens wrote, 'It's been the best of times, and it's been the worst of times.' First, the good things..."

Deb showed up again, still carrying the coffee pot. "You guys good for now?"

"We are Deb," Tom said. "Padre, care to bless this meal?" A cry from a familiar voice calling for more coffee and Deb left after another eye roll.

He began, "Almighty Father, Creator God, bless this food to our bodies. Bless all who come in here with peace, real peace that can come only through the forgiveness of sin through Jesus Christ. Amen."

"Amen. I could use some peace today."

"Okay," Padre said. "How's about we chow down, and then you tell me what's going good and what's not. Padre knows best, you know?"

"Fair enough," Tom said.

The two men wolfed down the hearty meal between a smidgen of small talk mainly about the weather. They quickly finished. Deb came around, took their plates, and then poured more coffee in their cups. The familiar voice sounded again, and Deb left to fill yet another cup for him.

“Now, how about you start with what's going right in your life, and you leave the bad stuff for last?” Padre said.

Tom sighed. “The good stuff? I have a wife that loves me madly, a new miracle daughter who's growing like a weed and astounding her doctors, and the bottled water business couldn't be better. The guys are working overtime, and I may have to hire a new driver soon to keep up with the increased business. So I guess I have a lot to be thankful for."

“Yes, it sounds like you do. Great blessings have come your way. But I see that look in your eyes. There’re big problems too.”

Tom nodded. "There are. There’re times I think I'm going crazy. It's got to be the PTSD and stress. This fellow who calls himself the Benefactor is still out there somewhere. I look over my shoulder, sometimes expecting him to be there. And last night, I had this crazy dream. I was driving an old truck at night, hit a deer, and had to shoot it to kill it. I drove on down the Dans Run Road toward Patterson Creek, and you know the goat farm on the left about two miles out..."

“I do.”

“Well, as I drove by, the goat's stares spoke to me. They said, 'Murder, killer, assassin.’”

“This is getting weird.”

"Oh, you ain't heard nothing yet." Padre's eyebrows went up. Tom continued, "I drove on down the road in the dark and came to the lane that leads to the farm where I was nearly killed twice because of my knowledge or lack of it on Braddock's Gold payroll. I couldn't help myself and turned in. The old gate crossing the road opened for me, beckoning me in, and I went. And the gate's not automatic. I no more than got up to the farm when a big black SUV like those answer-to-no one government spooks drive, pulled up behind me. He got out."

"He?"

"The man who calls himself the Benefactor. He told me he wanted this to be over, and I said I did too. So I emptied the gun into him. He just stood there like nothing happened and laughed. He said, 'Do you think it's that easy to kill me?' A small flame started at his head and soon consumed him. He crumbled to ashes that fell in a heap, but a demon that looked like a Phoenix rose from it and flew away. I felt a presence behind me. It was him, and he said, 'Trust me. I will save you.' I awoke screaming, 'No, no, no.' Fortunately, Jo was up with the baby and not next to me where I might have harmed her while this episode was going on."

"You definitely have my attention Tom, but I feel there's still more."

"There is. I was thinking about this on the way here. About a half-mile from here, a big deer came up into the road and stood there, glaring at me. And its eyes spoke to me, 'Murder, killer, assassin.' At the very last moment, it leaped away like a ghost. I was so shaken; I nearly wrecked the truck. I don't know what all this means. Am I going crazy or what?"

Tom's eyes begged for an answer. Padre was quiet as he stroked his chin. "I'm no psychiatrist, but I think I know acute stress when I see it. I think there's something else going on here too on a spiritual level, and I'm not sure what. It seems like the devil's after you, and there seems to a hidden message, one that I'm not sure of.

That's super heavy-duty stress to me, and I think I have a prescription for it. It's the best medicine I know."

"Give it to me. I need it triple strength."

"You will recognize it, Philippians 4, Paul's letter to the people of Philippi.

"Tom, it helped back then, and it'll help you today. The only difference is today we're all going faster and making more noise doing it. Everyone on earth sees it. Mahatma Gandhi commented that there was more to life than increasing its speed. Many others have said the same. Paul's words in Philippians are what got me through the last few months."

"I'm all ears, Padre. Preach on."

"The only way I know to turn stress into peace is by claiming the peace of God. Pray to the Man. Give all that junk to Jesus. You say, 'Jesus, You got to deal with this. It's more than I can handle. This burden's bigger than me.' And I know it's easier said than done. Been there. Tom, peace in your heart depends on what's going on in your head. You have to meditate on truth, justice, purity, things of good report.

"Tom, you, and me too, can get into a spiral of depression. It will spread like wildfire if you let it. Think of things that make you joyful. It makes others around you happier. Happiness is contagious."

"Padre, I'm feeling some better already. Preach on. I need it."

"Tom, you can't do this in your own power. Do it in the power of God. Philippians 4:13 says, 'I can do all things through Christ who strengthens me.' We get to thinking we're the focal point of the universe and that the whole world's against us. Instead of looking inward, look outward to those around you and to the good

Lord up above. You've been blessed with so much, a beautiful wife, a new baby, and growing business. Be content with what you have, and God will take care of the rest.

"Tom, I wish I could say I've done all this right the first time, but I haven't, and will probably mess up again and have to be reminded of all this myself. I just wish I could learn it all the first time and not have to repeat it again."

"Amen to that," Tom said.

"Remember, I can do all things through Christ who strengthens me. You can't really do much in your own strength. Be joyful. Old Nehemiah said it this way, 'The joy of the Lord is my strength.'"

"That's Nehemiah 8:10 you're quoting. Great verse."

Padre continued, "God will provide a way for you and me. Philippians 4:19 says, 'God will provide *all* our needs through his riches in glory.' He has an endless supply in His heavenly storehouses."

Tom said, "You're making me feel better already. I think this was a divine appointment today. It was what I needed. Thank you."

"Any time for a friend. I'm just sorry I didn't contact you sooner. I felt guilty about staying away."

"All's forgiven on that account Padre, and I seem to have forgotten my wallet. Can you pick up the tab?"

"You're not fooling with me on this, are you? You really did forget your wallet?"

"I did. My wallet with my money and driver's license are in my pants lying on the floor by the bed in my bedroom. I grabbed the first pair I found in the dresser, and all I have are my keys. I found them when I stepped on them in the dark. I'll be hurtin' if I get stopped by the cops."

"You'll probably know him, and he'll laugh it off, you forgetting your wallet and driver's license."

"True, but my breakfast still needs to be paid for. Aren't you forgetting that?"

"Your lucky day, Tom. God will provide. Padre will pick up the tab and let you skate this time, but it's your turn next time."

"Sounds fair enough to me. Thanks"

The men got up to leave. Padre left a good-sized tip for Deb and then paid the bill. He walked out to where Tom was waiting for him. Tom said, "You know Padre, a song started running through my head."

"Which one was that?"

"God leads us along. Some through the waters, some through the valley in the darkness of night, some through the fire, but all through the blood, some through great sorrows, but He's always there, in the night season and all the day long."

"Truer words have no man spoken. You be alright now?"

"I think so. Thank you for sharing with me."

"You're welcome. Let's try to meet more often."

"I'd like that."

"One last thing, after the good words, let me remind you that God always answers prayers, yours and mine, and we may not like it always. Sometimes He says go. Sometimes He says slow, and sometimes he says no. Remember, Paul asked thrice to be relieved of his thorn in the flesh, and God told him no? His grace was sufficient for him. God may tell you this is something you have to live with and live through. I know you've thought of that."

"I have. I wouldn't be looking forward to it, but God has His reasons. Maybe He's trying to teach me something, or it's necessary for some unfulfilled business He has with me. As you said, His grace is sufficient, and I can count on that. Okay?"

"Okay Tom, now I have to run. Confessions to hear and sinners to scare the living hell out of."

Tom laughed. "See you later, my friend. Thanks for giving me some joy and hope, and breakfast too."

The two men hugged and then went their separate ways. Padre left the parking lot first and was out of sight. Cars continued to pass behind Tom in the parking lot. He looked forward and saw something that frightened him. A deer peeked around the corner of a nearby house. It looked at him, and then calmly walked away. A cold chill went up his spine. What else was waiting for him today and the days ahead?

He knelt his head to pray. Oh Lord, what are You waiting on? How long for justice to be done? I cry out, Lord, but are You listening? Why is nothing happening? How long must I wait? Oh Lord, help me to be like Habakkuk. Hear my voice. Lighten my burden. I know You will answer at precisely the right time in accordance to Your perfect plan and purposes. I know, You have the final word.

Oh Lord, I don't have this all figured out. I'm still learning, and I still suffer the same old struggles to trust You in the here and now again and again. Let these struggles be reasons to get to know

You better and not doubt Your goodness and love. Help me trust You, and may this challenge bring wisdom and boldness.

All power belongs to You and You alone. You order the movement of Your Sun, and it conquers the darkness at the correct time. You said if we called out to You, You would answer. My heart is weary. Lord, please make it soon. Amen

He sighed and looked up — no deer. He pulled out onto WV Route 28 and headed toward home. *How long, oh Lord? How long?*

Chapter 9

Fall 1776

John Phares looked at the sun as it peeked over the hills to the east. A cold windy breeze made him draw his coat around him tighter. Old Man Winter was coming soon; he could tell as surely as day follows night. Early snow was possible. The trees were bare, and fallen leaves covered the ground. The woolly bears were dark and furry. The courier sent by General George Washington, John's longtime friend and confidante, had delivered a letter to him that told of some of the horrible difficulties the men and women who followed the army were experiencing: little shelter from the coming cold, poor food if any, and lots of sickness and deaths from the conditions. Only months ago, the colonists had cheered as news of the signing of the Declaration of Independence had spread.

From John's own experiences as a member of English General Braddock's failed expedition, he knew war was hell, but more soldiers fell from field conditions than battle. Washington's letter instructed John to remain on the western frontier and continue to head the local militia. The General and other likeminded men still feared an attack from the west by the British and their many Indian allies. Cold and snow should keep that threat low during the winter, but with the following spring, the genuine threat would return.

Rivers ran low from the dry fall months of this waning year. He prayed for heavy snow that would slow or stop any invading force. So far, the few attacks from the British and their Indian allies had been to the far west in the Ohio River Valley.

The courier filled in the blanks in Washington's letter. The American forces were in dire straits. General Washington's campaign in New York had been a disaster. The British and their Hessian mercenaries now controlled large parts of three states. Starvation, sickness, warfare, and exposure had taken the lives of thousands of soldiers the Colonials could not spare. Somehow Washington was holding the ragtag army together. Rumors of military arms and financial help from the British's traditional enemy, the French, circulated in the camp. This hope helped also. Perhaps, it would be coming soon. It was desperately needed. Maybe the French were holding off until they saw more signs that the American rebellion could succeed. After a day's rest, some good food prepared by Jenny, John's wife of many years, the courier had continued to the forts west in the mountains. The general desperately needed information on conditions at those locations so he could make his plans against the British in the east. If things were not going well on the western front, resources would have to be sent, and he had none to spare.

The letter sealed with wax and stamped with the general's signet ring print in it had not been tampered with. He recognized the Washington family's crest with a winged griffin coming out of a crown. The letter was authentic. He checked for hidden or invisible messages but found none. Besides the description of the horrible conditions at the camp, Washington had included a veiled and coded message he knew John would understand. Though never stated outright, the general had requested help that only John could provide. John understood. The army needed finances badly.

Washington had been a true friend, and John knew he would send help.

A little smile came to John's face as he thought of how mad King George III would be if he knew his grandfather's gold, lost years earlier when General Braddock was defeated, would be used to finance an army against him. This would be John's second gift of Braddock's Gold to Washington. The first had been just before the fighting in the war had broken out, and now again, he would help his friend from the Tidewater. Washington could be a little stuffy at times. John believed that to be from his upbringing among the upper crust aristocracy. Times roughing it on the frontier among the hard-working, hard-drinking, and independent-minded Scots and Irish had given Washington an appreciation of the people there. The industry of German immigrants who turned forested lands into productive farms had also been admired. He knew Washington was one who liked to impress those around him, and they were rarely disappointed.

A horse whinnied, and John turned to see his teenage daughter Jasmine in the dawning sunlight, leading the chestnut mare from the barn. John had purchased the horse from a man named Justin Morgan, who was passing through. He was a horse buyer and breeder and in need of money. The mare had caught John's eye from the first time he saw her. The two men worked out a fair agreement, shook on it, and the compact horse with a clean build, and powerfully muscled hindquarters had become John's own for all of a half-hour before Jasmine saw her, claimed her, and named her Red Queen. He had wanted the chestnut for himself, but the two bonded like sisters, and there would be no separating them.

"How's the Queen today, Jasmine?" he asked though he already knew the answer from one look at the mare.

"Right as rain can be, Paw. She's saddled up, ready to go. I got what I need for the journey, and I'll take good care of the cargo. I'll see that Uncle George gets it, or I'll die trying."

"I bet you will, too. And you be respectful when you see General Washington and address him properly, you hear? Uncle George is a name you must only use when others are not around."

"I will, Paw. You know me better than that. You explained how important this cargo is to the cause."

John said no more as he watched his oldest climb into the saddle on the powerful horse with the short back. *My, how she had grown. It seemed like just yesterday midwife Granny Wagoner had delivered her into this world.* He could still remember the old woman's words, "My, oh my. That little gal's something, Mister Phares. Long, lean, and muscular. Good set of lungs to match that head of red hair. That girls gonna grow up and be somebody. I can just feel it, John. I can feel it."

It wasn't too long afterward, Mrs. Wagoner took sick and died. John had helped dig her grave in the little family plot on the knoll in the pasture east of the old cabin the Wagoner family called home. After a short service with family and neighbors, she was buried in a rough pine and poplar coffin next to two of her children who had died in their youth. Her eldest daughter had become the new midwife and delivered all the rest of John and Jenny's children, along with many others in the growing community.

"Paw, do you think Uncle George will know me? I was a whole lot younger and smaller and don't look like I do now."

"You won't get straight in to see him. You'll have to go through his sentinel guards. The bloody British have a price on his head and would love him dead. If he dies, I think the rebellion could collapse. I think everyone knows that. You tell the guards you're there with a message and package from John Phares, and only General Washington's eyes are to see them."

"And if they don't listen?"

"You do what I said. If that fails, show them the letter from General Washington that gives J. Phares permission to pass all guard directly to Excellency General Washington without delay. And if that fails, tell them you came directly from Colonel Phares himself, a personal friend and confidante of General Washington, and you are to shoot and kill anyone who interferes. If they make any hostile moves toward you, forget giving them a chance. Maim and kill them if necessary, understand?"

"Yes, Paw."

"And I know you are quite capable of doing just that."

"Yes, Paw, and you know I would, too. I may be young, but I know how much is riding on me getting the go…, getting the cargo to General Washington."

"Always call it cargo, Jasmine. Never use the word gold. Men have been known to kill their own brothers for gold."

"Yes, Paw. I won't make that mistake again ever. You can count on me."

"I know I can. That's why I picked you to go. Your brother may be a great farmer, but he's no horseman or marksman like you are."

"I owe that all to you and Injun Joe."

Injun Joe. John smiled as he thought of the debt he owed to Injun Joe. He'd been like a member of the family. He refused ever to sleep in the old family cabin even during the worst of cold. If not for his bravery and sacrifice, all John's family would have died horrible deaths at the hands of the two bandits who had surprised the family while John was away.

"I still miss him, Paw. He was my best friend and taught me so much about being a hunter and warrior."

"I know he did, though it drove your mother crazy. She wanted a daughter who would be a homemaker like she is."

"I know, Paw. I think God broke the mold after He made me."

"He had a good reason, don't you think?"

"Yes, He did. Don't think this world is ready for too many more like me."

He nodded. If not for the warrior's mindset she had learned from him, the family would not have survived. After Injun Joe had killed the first bandit, he'd been killed by the second. While the second was distracted, Jasmine had taken a four-pronged wooden hay rake and run it clear through the last bandit just below his ribs.

"I sure hope some of his ashes you placed in Patterson Creek make it all the way down the Potomac to the eastern ocean he wanted so bad to see."

"I do too, Jasmine. He would have liked that."

"You know Paw; I've always felt closer to you and man work than woman's work. Don't get me wrong. I love my mom, but I'm just not the homebody girl she wanted, and I never will be."

"I know Jasmine, and your maw knows that too, even if it grates on her and makes her feel somehow she failed with you."

"I am who I am, Paw, and always will be."

John’s mind drifted off to a time some years ago shortly after Injun Joe's death. He knew there had been trouble of some sort between Jenny and Jasmine. Their temperament was too much alike, and the friction would turn to fire someday, though he could not have made up the story of how it happened if he tried. He had been out in the barn when the caterwauling had started. As he ran out of the barn, he nearly fell when he stepped in fresh manure. He quickly recovered and raced toward the tumult in front of the house. There he found Jasmine and her mother screaming at each other, and Jasmine was as naked as the day she was born. Jenny was facing him, and Jasmine had her bare backside to him. "What's going on?" he remembered yelling.

Jenny said, “She says she’s not wearing any more clothes ever.”

Jasmine turned slightly and saw her father. She drew up her hands in an attempt to cover herself.

“Is that so, Jasmine?” he asked.

“NO! I said I wasn’t ever wearing dresses ever again. I want to wear britches and shirts, and I ain’t never gonna wear a dress again if it kills me.”

“You talk to her, John. I might as well talk to a tree. You talk some sense into her.” She stormed off into the house, leaving John with his naked daughter.

For a moment, he did not know what to say. “Jasmine, are you really that determined to never wear a dress that you would rather go naked for the rest of your life?”

She looked over her bare shoulder at him. “I would. I hate dresses. I want clothes like you wear. Besides, if God made me born naked, being naked must have been good enough for Him. Wasn't Adam and Eve created naked in the beginning?"

John could see he would get nowhere with his daughter, especially if she started bringing up the Bible. She was more versed in it that he was because of the time she had spent learning readin' from her mother. An idea came to him. "Jasmine, you can have my old clothes your maw was goin' to use as rags, breeches, and shirt for now, but if you want clothes that fit and aren't full of holes, you'll have to make your own. How does that sound?"

John could tell she was becoming very self-conscious of her nakedness. She thought for a quick second. "Okay. It's a deal."

John grinned at his cleverness. "You wait right here, and I'll find my old clothes. Don't go anywhere."

"I won't," she said sheepishly.

John went into the house and found his old clothes in the rag pile, walked outside, and waited. Jenny came to him, walking backward, and covering herself with her hands and arms. John placed his long old shirt over her head and pulled it down over her. It fell to mid-thigh. He handed her the breeches which she carefully put on. "Thanks, Paw," she said. "You're the best." She hugged him and began to walk away in her new coverings.

"Jasmine, there is one more thing."

"What's that, Paw?" He whispered something in her ear. After that, she said, "I knew there had to be a catch. Okay, Paw, I can do that."

John walked back into the old cabin. Jenny met him with a scowl on her face and her hands on her hips. "So, she wins just like that?"

“Everyone wins,” he said.

She looked at him from the corner of her eye, not believing. “How so?”

“You know she’s as stubborn as you are.”

“More so than even me. More like a mule. A stubborn, bull-headed mule at that.”

John knew better, but let it slide. "She gets my old stuff, and it covers her nakedness now. I told her if she wanted proper clothes, she would have to make them herself. You wouldn't do it. She must, and she agreed."

"John, you're a scoundrel, and I love you. You could make a deal with Old Scratch himself and come out on top."

“The best deal I ever made was when I purchased your indentured servant papers from Durham.”

“It will be too soon if I ever hear his name again.”

“And I shall never bring that scoundrel up again.”

John’s thoughts and gaze went back on his daughter. Jasmine was as tall as him and lean as lean could be. Her breasts were small, and her hips slender. The baggy clothes cloaked her shape. Her face had no beard, but the army was taking males of any age, even those not ready to shave. She could easily pass as a young boy or maybe even a young man.

“Paw? Paw? Are you alright? You looked like you done drifted off somewheres far, far away.”

“Guess I did. Something you said brought up old memories.”

"Paw, I guess I better get going. We're burning daylight, and I've got a long way to go. I better get moving." She nudged the horse, and she began to move slowly.

"I love you, Jasmine."

The horse stopped, and she looked around. "And I love you too, Paw."

“Your Maw loves you too, Jasmine.”

“I know Paw. Tell her I love her too.”

“I will. She knows.” John thought he saw her fight back a tear as she turned.

“Gotta go.” And like the wind, she was off. She quickly disappeared down the path from the cabin to the crossroads and through the trees that lined the road headed east. John listened to the sound of the horse’s familiar gait as it became less and less and finally could not be heard.

He was sorry to see Jasmine go, but she was the one cut out for this task. She would be safe, as safe as was possible. He had heard tales of how she had made a gang of rabble back down in town recently. They’d been harassing her, a young woman in men's clothes. One said he would ride that filly and ride her hard. Quick as a flash, a big and razor-sharp knife she pulled from her under her hunting frock made him change his mind. That and the fact she’d told the big man if he really was a man, she would turn him into a gelding if he came a step closer. She had taken a half step forward when the men ran out the door like a she-demon was after them. She stood in the doorway as the men hastily jumped on their horses and galloped off. The storekeeper said she cut her palm slightly and drew blood. She told him once she had pulled the knife, blood must be spilled before it was returned to the sheath. A brave and mighty warrior had taught her that. The story spread, and no man had bothered her since. Ambush was the only thing that bothered him, and there was little that could be done to avoid it except extreme vigilance. And she was always cautious, especially when alone.

The sun was rising rapidly as he strapped down the metal box containing the rest of the gold he had recovered from the old swivel gun where he had placed it years ago. He rode down the hill on the old but strong plow mule, across the dirt road, and into the flat land where Dennison Run and Dans Run merged before entering Patterson Creek. He pulled up a sycamore sapling growing in the rocks along the stream and carried it with him. In the flat bottomland, he dug a hole and buried the box with the gold coins inside. He was getting too old to go traipsing off in need of the gold he had buried farther away. In a way, John hoped that ole King George III would find out the revolution by the colonists was being funded with English gold, Braddock's Gold. John had never forgiven them for what they had done to their neighbors in Scotland and Ireland, and this would be payback. Oh, how he wished he could see the King's red face. Maybe someday, he would.

Chapter 10

Berean Church, Fort Ashby, WV, 1998

"Damn these gnats," Dutch growled under his breath. He tried not to use foul language. His wife had been fussing at him for that. She was his second wife and younger. His hard living and hard ways had chased the first one off. She had enough and looking back on it, Dutch couldn't blame her. Some of his good old days had been pretty bad. He was glad for a second chance. They hadn't planned on children, but sometimes those things happened. Their small son had been repeating what he had heard his father say, and his wife did not like it at all. Dutch knew she was right. He wanted to get it right this time around. He bit his tongue as even fouler thoughts about the bugs crossed his mind. Besides, he was working at a church, his church, and it just didn't seem proper to curse here.

Almost a year ago at this very church, he'd done something he thought was impossible, given his life to the Lord. He'd not been a bad character. No one had ever questioned his honesty, but he had a roughness about him that you find in many construction workers, tough and thorny on the outside, but tender on the inside like a sabra cactus. His wife had started going to the church, and he'd seen a change in her. The emptiness she had inside had been filled with joy and love, and he wanted what she had. He was so glad the Lord took people just as they were. He'd been a real piece of work and had every bad habit common to construction workers plus a few more. The Lord had been working on him in the last year and was slowly cleaning up his language. It had not been easy on either of them.

He stopped his digging with the orange Kubota backhoe and covered himself with Off Insect Repellant containing lots of DEET. He always carried some with him. Years of experience working outside had taught him a bundle. What did he expect anyway? There was productive cow pasture all around him, and with cows came cow pies and with cow pies came gnats and flies, but today it was merely a plague of gnats of almost biblical proportion. They weren't very big, but their number was many as they flew around him. "Blessed gnats," he said with a snarl that made the words sound like Christian cussing if Christians cussed. "Blessed gnats," he repeated. Another thing he had learned was always to bring more clothes than you need. You can always take it off, but you can't put on what you don't have.

He could have been making a lot more than what he was charging to put in the new larger septic tank and field. On the job as an Operating Engineer, he got union wages and benefits, and he used the company's equipment, not his own as he was today. All in all, he guessed he was doing this for about minimum wages with what he was charging the church, but he felt it was well worth it considering the debt of sin and guilt the Lord had paid forward for him.

The congregation of the little yellow Baptist church had been meeting in their gym and fellowship hall since the fire a year ago. The origin had been suspicious, but police had been unable to make an arrest in the ongoing case. With the insurance money, volunteer help, and the assistance of a church building mission group, Continental Building Missions, the new sanctuary had been dried in, and soon, the work on the interior would begin. With that goal reached, the workmen and their families who traveled with them and lived in the travel trailers set up on the church property had taken a well-earned vacation back home, wherever that was.

He was the only one there today asides from the pastor who was inside the unfinished church catching up on sermons and paperwork. Digging had been going smoothly. He'd hit few roots from the nearby trees as he dug the ditches for the new drain field. From years of work and observing various soils, he knew there should be no surprises with drainage here. Still, the state demanded there be reserve land set aside if the new field was inadequate and did not work as expected. He moved the backhoe to where the deep hole for the septic tank was to go. With the two outriggers down, he spun the seat around and began to dig. Almost immediately, he hit roots, lots of large thick and sturdy roots. Then he remembered that an old and colossal sycamore tree had grown here. About the time he started coming to the church with his wife, an intense summer storm everyone in the community would remember for years because of the vicious winds and abundant lightning had hit. The entire top of the old tree came down after being hit by the lighting and then further demolished by the hurricane-force winds. Just his luck, they wanted the septic tank in probably the worse choice of a spot on the entire property. *Sometimes Lady Luck shines on you, and sometimes it doesn't.* He'd agreed to put the tank in and that he would do, big and lousy tree roots or not.

The roots would be a challenge, but he had faced worse. He would getter done one way or the other. He had been in a lot of places and worked a lot of big jobs. The Jennings Randolph Dam job came to mind. He had been the one to discover the igneous rock stratus and the so-called "waffle" rock with the checkerboard pattern. Dutch had always been a curious man, and this led him on a quest of discovery. In the Appalachian Mountains he called home, he had never thought of as having any volcanic characteristics, but he learned of two volcanic cones in nearby Virginia-the Monterey Mole

Hill and Trimble Knob. Mt. Rogers in Grayson Highland State Park, the highest place in Virginia at over a mile high, was said to be volcanic by geologists. There were also numerous warm and hot springs in the mountain chain running up the east coast of America. Now he understood why there were sometimes earthquakes in the area, some of which were real attention grabbers.

He tore away at the tree roots one by one until only a taproot where the tree had stood remained. Dutch had it exposed on all four sides. He slid the bucket carefully down on the far side of the stump and pulled the lever to place the bucket under it. Next, he would use the strong arm pistons to pull it out. Gingerly, he felt his way along. So far, so good. With a pop, the roots left holding the stump snapped, and a small satisfied smile came to his face. He turned the big arm over to the side and placed the stump on the ground. A sharp metal sound caught his ear. Chink. He shook the stump with the machine's strong arm. Chink. There it was again.

He turned the engine to the machine off and stepped down from it. There was something rusty trapped in the roots. *A metal box, maybe?* He looked a little closer, and sure enough, he could see part of what he took to be an old, rusty box. The tree had grown around the box on three sides. Dutch went to his pickup and retrieved a round-nosed shovel and an ax. The shovel scooped up the heavy sedimentary soil, and with the ax, he chopped away at a small root in the way. He slipped as he took a hard hack at the root. The ax glanced off, and the business end struck the ancient box. It sank through the side and stuck. Broad-shouldered Dutch pulled hard on the ax. On a third massive yank, it came flying out much to the big man's surprise who nearly fell, but recovered with his man pride still intact.

Dutch looked inside the hole the ax had made and saw a little gold color shining. Carefully sticking his fingers in the opening, he pulled out something metal and heavy for its size. He spat on it and rubbed off the dirt. It was a coin of some sort. Whoever the person on it was, he or she had long hair, a noble chin and forehead, and eyes that appeared to Dutch to bulge somewhat.

He put the coin in his pocket and chopped away at the roots some more until he could free the box. He pulled it out and found it to be weighty, especially considering its size. Dutch worked the lid up, and his mouth dropped open. The box was full of gold coins of various sizes, but all seemed to have the same person on the front, or someone who looked very similar.

For an instant, he was tempted to carry the box to his truck and claim it as his own, but Dutch was an honest man, honest to a fault, and the idea quickly passed. No, this was not his, and he hated thieves. He closed the lid and shoved some loose dirt over the box. "That's sure a lot of money there," he said out loud to himself, "but it ain't mine."

He walked over to the church, stomped his feet on the new concrete porch on the unfinished church, and walked inside quickly. The pastor was sitting at a card table in a metal folding chair. A tall floor light with a long arm illuminated his work area. He jumped as Dutch's sudden appearance startled him. Even in the dim light, Pastor Richard could see a look of concern on the big man's face.

"Dutch, what's wrong? Are you hurt? What's going on, buddy?"

"You ain't ever gonna believe this Pastor, but I think I just found a treasure box under that old stump right where I was diggin' a hole for the new septic tank. I think it's full of gold."

"Dutch, I know you're a big kidder and love a practical joke, so don't think I'm going to fall for your trick, okay, buddy."

“No kidding, Pastor. This is for real. Cross my heart and hope to die.”

“Okay, I’ll go along with your prank. Let’s see what you found, haw haw.”

“Come on, then.”

Dutch hurried out to the dirt-covered box. Pastor Richard followed along wearily, looking for any others involved in the prank but saw no one. “Here it is, Pastor. Just like I said.”

He took his big hands and swept the loose soil away from the old box. “See? Just like I said.”

“Yeah, right. Just like you said. An old box. Yippy.”

“Honest Pastor, I ain’t kiddin’.” He opened the box, and the contents shined in the sun. Pastor Richard's sardonic grin dropped from his face. He fell to his knees next to Dutch, stuck his hand in the box and pulled out a handful of coins, and ran them through his fingers. One he put to his mouth and bite.

"You know something Dutch; this looks like the real McCoy. You weren't pulling my leg."

“Yessiree. Got any idea what it is and where it came from?”

He thought for a moment. “Yeah, I do on both accounts.” He gazed across the road at the old farmhouse where Dan Phares lived then turned to Dutch. "You need to keep this quiet. I think this is real, and it may well turn out to be a Pandora’s Box you found. Tell no one, not even your good wife. There’s people out there who would kill for this. We have to keep this a secret. I have a place I can keep this hidden, and I think I know who can tell me more about this, but you have to keep this our secret. Your find could endanger our lives and others."

A serious look came to Dutch's face. "It's that serious?"

“Serious as a heart attack. People have died for far less.”

“So, what do we do right now?”

"Let me take care of the box, and you go back to work on the septic system. The least things seem out of the ordinary here; the less suspicion will be aroused. I think that's our best course of action. You aren't too spooked to go back to work and do it safely, are you?"

Dutch gave his best macho face. “I was with the Marines on operations that officially never happened. I don't scare too easy, and I know when to keep my mouth shut. You can count on me.”

“Good, I’ll carry the box over to the church and find a place for it now till I can get it in a safe place.” He picked up the box. “My, this is heavy, very heavy.”

“I told you so. Need any help with it, Pastor?”

“I’ll manage. Thanks, just the same. Let’s try to pretend this did not happen.”

“Gotcha, Pastor. Nothing to see here. Move along.”

Dutch hopped up on the backhoe and started it up as Pastor Richard lugged the heavy burden in the church to a temporary hiding place. He resumed digging the hole for the septic tank, but his mind was elsewhere as he worked. Dutch could keep his mouth shut, but what, oh what, had he found and how much trouble could one old box cause? He wasn’t sure he wanted to find out.

Chapter 11

Tom looked out the window of his delivery truck. The cold rain, fog, and grey sky matched his mood. What else could go wrong today? The baby had cried half the night. Joann suspected an earache and had taken her to the doctor. God only knew how long she would be there. Tom awoke with a headache and his sinuses acting up. They had argued over what Tom knew was next to nothing. Just two people feeling rotten and prickly. Not a good combination, and then it had gotten worse. A fully loaded truck refused to start. It had to be unloaded and reloaded on another one. Jerry was not present at the starting time. He called in an hour late sick, sick as a dog, sick as a sick dog. Said he was going from both ends. Sitting on the toilet with diarrhea and throwing up in a trash can. At least there was one person in this world feeling worse than he did.

Tom cruised the narrow road north into Ridgeley, West Virginia. The guardrail on the downhill side started right where the pavement ended, and the mountainside began on the other side, also where the pavement ended. It was not a road to make a mistake on. He squeezed past a yellow school bus heading the other way with only inches to spare. Tom slowed for the speed trap at the foot of the mountain that welcomed all into Ridgeley. The Knobley Mountain Bottled Water truck crept through the small town, always sure to stay below the posted speed limit. The truck barely slipped under the low Western Maryland Railroad bridge. A sharp right followed by another sharp left and he crossed the blue bridge over the Potomac River into Maryland.

At the light, he took a left on old Route 220 and was soon at Sheetz store for a delivery. He backed the truck into the loading area, set the brake, and turned off the ignition. A face hidden by a hoodie leaped to the window. Tom jumped back away from the staring face, partially obscured by straggly brown hair. It stared at him for a moment and then spoke. “Tom, it’s me. I’ve been expecting you.”

His heart pounded in his chest. “Who’s me?”

A dirty hand pulled the hoodie off the head. “See? It’s me. Carole.”

Tom exhaled, much relieved. “Carole, you like to scared me to death. If I was a cat, you would have just cost me two of my nine lives.”

“Sorry,” she said. “Crazy Carole has a way of doing that. I’m sorry, Tom. Could you buy me breakfast? I haven’t eaten since noon yesterday. Kinda hungry. Please?”

Crazy Carole, yes, he knew who she was, one of the homeless people with mental health problems every town has. Crazy Carole, he hadn’t seen her for a while. Wonder what she’s been up to? Guess he was going to find out.

“Okay, Carole. You know me well. I’m always there if you need a meal.”

“Could we eat before you drop your load here?”

“Sure, you want the usual?”

“Yeah, chicken biscuit, hash browns, and coffee, black. No milk or sugar.”

“Sounds good, Carole. Let’s go.”

Tom got out of the truck and headed toward the store entrance with Carole following close behind. He opened the door for her. “Thanks, Tom. It’s always nice to be treated like a lady, not human garbage.”

"Find a seat for us, and I'll get the food."

“Sure thing. Thanks so much, Tom.”

There was no line at the counter. Tom gave the order to the young woman behind the counter and paid her. He watched as she grabbed the items he ordered, bagged them, and gave it to him. “Thanks,” he said.

“Always good to see you well, Mr. Kenney.”

Surprised, Tom asked, “Sorry. I can’t say I remember you. How do I know you?”

“I was a nurse over at the Cumberland Veteran’s Hospital till the cutbacks. I cared for you last time you were there. My name's Anna, Anna Jenkins."

“Sorry, I don’t remember you.”

“That’s okay. You were kind of out of it. That PTSD thing.”

“Yeah, wish I could beat it.”

“I know. I worked with a lot of fellows who have it and a few gals, too.”

“So, they cut you loose. VA's not got enough people, and they're cutting back. It seems like the vets are always getting cheated out of what they earned.”

“Ain’t that the truth?”

“So, what are you doing working at Sheetz?”

“Temporary job to hold me over till I find another nursing job. It’s a little tight, but I’ll get by. I’ve learned to be content whatever my lot, whatever my situation?”

“That sounds like the apostle Paul. Are you a Christian?”

“Yep. I don’t know what I’d do without my faith. Don’t get me wrong. It was a real downer when I got the pink slip. Sure wasn’t expecting it. I cried a little, pulled up my big girl britches, and moved on.”

“Wish I could do the same with the PTSD.”

"Some things are harder than others, Mr. Kenney. They don't always work out as we would like. Old Paul wanted the Lord to get rid of his ‘thorn in the flesh' problem, and He didn't. You ever thought it might be like that?"

"Yeah, I've thought of that. Like Paul, I would like to be rid of it, but as you say, it's up to the good Lord." He paused. "Are you a psychiatrist too?"

“Nah. I used to tend bar in the bad old days before Jesus set me on the straight and narrow. I learned to read people really well back then. Ain’t nothing wasted in this journey called life. Everything has a reason and a purpose. I wouldn’t be who I am today if it wasn’t for all the storms I’ve gone through.”

A man walked up behind Tom and asked, “Is this where I order?”

Tom said, “Yes, it is. Thank you, Anna, for your kind words. Great words of advice. Thanks.”

"Anytime," she said. "Stop in again."

Tom walked away feeling better. He turned around and saw the smiling Anna taking the man's order. *Perhaps, she was right. Be content wherever you are. In times of plenty or when times are lean. In the times going good or not going good. Easy to mouth, but hard to live.*

"Hey, Tom. Did you get lost?" Carole called from the nearby seat.

"Sorry. I was distracted by some good vibes."

He sat down, gave a quick blessing, and the two chowed down on the food. Carole practically inhaled the large biscuit and hash browns. She sipped at her steaming coffee. Tom looked at her. "Boy, oh boy. You sure were hungry."

"Yup. I really thank you for this. Would it be too much to ask for another?"

"No, it wouldn't." He handed her a five-dollar bill. "Get what you want and keep the change."

"Thanks, Tom. You've always been so good to me, never asking for anything in exchange." She got up out of her seat, hugged the surprised man, and went to the counter.

Tom couldn't explain it, but he felt a chill about him. *Probably someone opened the door.*

Carole was soon back with her food. She sat down, opened the wrapper up, took a bite, chewed, and spoke through the full mouth. "He's here."

"Who's here?"

"The Death Angel is sitting next to me and looking at you."

Once before in this same store, she had announced the same. He thought back to that day. Knowing her mental state, he did not believe her until she began to tell him things about his life she couldn't possibly know. She said she was only repeating what the Death Angel had said. And he believed her then and now.

“Carole, you sure know how to get my attention. How’s he dressed today? Same as last time? Does he have any information he cares to share today?”

“Well, he’s dressed the same as usual. Dark suit, white shirt, black bow tie, and white gloves. Oh, I forgot the sunglasses.”

“Sunglasses?”

"Yeah, kind of like those cool, expensive ones you see the Hollywood stars wearing. He says his jet black eyes freaked out some of the people he came to get. With the sunglasses, they seemed to accept their impending demise better.”

“Is he here for me today?”

“He says no. You’re not on today’s list.”

“How about tomorrow’s?”

“He says he won’t have it till tomorrow.”

Tom said, “Guess that’s why they call today the ‘present.’ Tomorrow may never come.”

“He said, ‘Just desserts.’” She smiled.

“Wonder what he meant by that?”

“Remember I told you about the woman who molested me at the mental health care center? She’s dead. She got her just desserts.”

"Now, I recall. The last time we were in this same spot, he said, 'just desserts' and took off." He thought for a moment. "Yeah, I remember seeing the picture on the front page of the Cumberland Times-News. Her car was smashed under the back of that McDonald's truck, and it had a big promotion painting on the side that read, 'Just Desserts.'"

"Exactly. He was right on the money."

"The Good Books says all that is hidden shall be revealed. You reap what you sow."

She said, "Some people call it karma."

"They do. Many religions have a similar idea on this. Ever secular people say, 'What goes around comes around.' Does he have anything else to say?"

"He said it will soon be over."

There was no way for Tom to hide the shocked look on his face. "What will soon be over? What is this It? Did he say anything more?"

"That's all he said. Nothing more."

Tom's mind raced. *What was this, "It?" His life? The charade with this nemesis who called himself the Benefactor? Or something else?*

"Ask him what 'it' is? I need to know. Please." There was silence. "Well?" Tom asked. "What did he say?"

"Nothing. He said nothing."

Tom looked at the empty seat and said, "Please."

Carole sighed. "He says you'll find out soon enough."

"Why can't I see him? He's so real to you?"

"Cause you're not crazy. His secrets are safe with me. No one believes what a crazy person says or does or sees. Maybe you should be happy you can't see him. Being crazy isn't all it's cracked up to be, Tom."

Tom lowered his eyes from hers to the table. Perhaps she was right. He opened his mouth to speak, but Carole cut him off. "He's gone."

"Carole, did I chase him off?"

"No, he said his coffee break was over. Had to get back to work."

"Did he really say that?"

"He did, but I think he was tired of your questions and wanted to go He's not one for humor, unless it's black, pun intended."

"Yeah, I think you're right. Bet he doesn't even like coffee, even coffee as black as you say he is or his humor."

Carole said, "What do you think he meant? He was right on about the 'Just Desserts.'"

"I can guess for what it's worth, but I think I'll find out. Soon."

Chapter 12

December 1776, Eastern Pennsylvania

Jasmine Phares was relieved when she saw the campfires in the army camp some miles east of Philadelphia. She'd had a rather uneventful journey from her home just south of the village of Cumberland in western Maryland. The people she'd met along her journey had shied away from her and seemed more interested in minding their own business than talking, which was fine with her. Curious people could be dangerous people looking to somehow take advantage of another. Numerous times, she'd had to stop at taverns and inns to ask directions east. It had taken her a full twenty days to reach the camp. She was tired of sleeping outside on the ground and guarding her cargo. Maybe tonight, she could stay in a house in a real bed or at least in a barn on some straw with the animals.

Jasmine had been stopped at the perimeter of the camp by a thin sentry in a worn and holey frock. He wore no shoes. She showed him the papers from General Washington. He showed little interest and directed her toward the general's location. The camp was a hodge-podge of well-worn tents and lean-to shelters most with rag-tag soldiers trying to stay warm around small fires. Jasmine had not expected the camp to be much in quality, but its poverty shocked her. If this was the rebellion's best hope, the rebels were in deep trouble. The men around the shelters paid her little mind, but one woman, probably a soldier's wife, took a long gaze at her. Jasmine was curious as to why she was being stared at, but she continued through the camp to the big house that had to be where the commander had his headquarters. A stern-looking sentry with a long and new scar on his chin that sprouted a few long strands of whiskers stopped her near the house. He demanded of the stranger, "State your business or be gone before I shoot you."

Jasmine gave him a cold stare. "I have business with the general. He requested my presence. I have paperwork from His Excellency I can show you. I have it inside my haversack. Would you like to see it?"

"Yes, and move your hands slowly. I'll shoot you without hesitation if you try anything funny."

Her eyes grew with intensity, and she said, "I'll do as you say, and I've no intention of harming His Excellency or dying today." Carefully and slowly, she unbuttoned the bag, slipped one hand in, and retrieved the letter. "Here it is. You'll see all is in order." She relaxed and handed him the paper.

He took it from her hand, looked at it quickly, barely taking his eyes off her. "Wait here," he growled and went to the door. He knocked at the door with the hand carrying the letter.

"Who is it?" came a voice from inside the house.

The sentry said, "We have a visitor who claims to have a letter from the general requesting his presence."

The voice inside the house said, "Is dat a fact? We shall see about dat." The door opened a little, and Jasmine could see a light-skinned black man with a ready pistol in his hand. He took the letter and shut the door tight.

"Now we wait," the sentry said. "For your sake, everything better be in order." Jasmine said nothing and did nothing to give the soldier a reason to shoot.

A minute passed. A crow cawed from somewhere. Jasmine could smell wood smoke mixed with something cooking. *A good meal would be a blessing*, she thought.

The door opened. The black man appeared. He still held the pistol ready if needed. "His Excellency says to admit you. Come in."

Jasmine dismounted deliberately. The situation was tense. She didn't want to escalate it by any sudden moves. She walked the few paces to the house, took two steps up, and entered the dark room. The door closed quickly behind her. It took a moment for her eyes to adjust. "Have a seat over there," the black man said sternly. "Don't you make no sudden moves if you know what's good for you." His pistol was pointed toward her chest. "General Washington will be here shortly."

Jasmine nodded she understood. She looked around the room. To her right was a small fireplace with a minimal fire, mainly glowing embers. The walls were bare. The only furniture in the room was the chair she was to sit in and a large secretary desk with a chair behind it. The room was cold, barely warmer than outside. The moments passed with nothing happening. A side door creaked as it opened quickly. General Washington entered the room. He carried the letter in his hand. His eyes carefully studied the buckskin-clad person standing in front of him. He said nothing and sat at the secretary.

He asked flatly, "How did this letter come into your possession, young man?"

Jasmine responded, "My father gave this to me along with some cargo you asked for."

“Your father? Who’s your father?”

“John Phares.”

“John Phares?” the general said. “That’s impossible.”

“Have I changed that much, Uncle George? Don’t you recognize me?”

“There’s only one person who would call me that.” He looked at the person across from him. “Jasmine?”

“Yes,” she smiled. “It’s me.”

He looked at her closely. He studied her eyes. “Why, it is you, Jasmine. You’ve changed so much since I last saw you. You must have shot up a foot in height. I can’t believe it’s you, but it is. You have your father’s eyes.”

“And my mother’s hair.”

Washington smiled. It was red like his. He spoke to the black man, "Billy, don't point the gun at our guest. I've known her father for close to twenty years. I still can't believe it's you. At first, I thought you were a young man."

“As did I,” Billy said.

Jasmine smiled, "It happens all the time, and I never saw any reason to correct the mistake. I've been able to do a lot of things a girl would never be allowed to do."

“Jasmine,” Washington said. “I’ve someone I’d like you to meet.” He exited the room. Jasmine could hear talking in the next room. Washington soon reappeared with a woman in a nice dress and a bonnet on her head. She had a shawl around her neck. “Martha,” he said. “This is the person I’ve told you about.”

Lady Washington smiled but looked somewhat confused. “It’s my pleasure to meet you, young man. My husband has said so many good things about you.”

Jasmine curtsied to Lady Washington. “It’s a pleasure to meet you too, mam. And I assure you, in spite of what you see, I’m just as much a woman as you.” Lady Washington looked confused. “Uncle George has spoken kindly about you the many times he visited my father’s homestead on the western frontier.”

"Uncle George, is it?" She looked at her husband. There was a surprise in her voice. "I'm a little taken back. First, I’ve mistaken your gender, and now my husband’s Uncle George? I do apologize for any harm I may have caused.”

“Lady Washington,” Jasmine said. “There’s no need for that. I know you meant no harm.”

“Have you eaten anything lately?” Lady Washington asked.

“No ma’am, I haven't. I haven't had a hot meal since I left home twenty days ago. I needed to keep an eye on the cargo His Excellency requested from my father, so I didn't take any meals in inns along the way here."

General Washington’s continence changed. “The cargo. You have the cargo I asked for?”

"Yes, sir. I told my father I would deliver it here or die trying,” Jasmine said. “I’ll get it.” She turned to leave the room.

General Washington said to Billy, “Billy, would you please help our guest with her cargo?”

Jasmine said, “No need for that. I can do it by myself, but thanks for the offer.” She turned and went outside, leaving the three.

General Washington said to Billy, "If that be the case, would you get the young lady a plate of food and something to drink?"

"Yes sir," he said. "Coming right up," and with that, Billy left the room.

Lady Washington said, "Oh my dear George, you're full of surprises today. Uncle George is it? And a lad that's a lady. A strong one at that. And what other surprises do you have up your sleeve?"

He held his hand to his mouth as if deep in thought and smiled. "Martha, you have no clue as to the ideas forming in my mind. Oh, the possibilities."

Chapter 13

As Jasmine stepped outside, the sentry turned to her. He said, “I’m sorry if I was gruff with you, young man. It’s my job to protect the general, and I take that seriously."

Jasmine said, "Yeah, I've heard the British have a high price on his head. You did ruffle my feathers, but I can understand your caution.” She proceeded to loosen the saddlebag containing her precious cargo.

“Let me help you with that,” the sentry said. She gave him a look that could kill.

“Maybe not,” he said.

“Thank you, but no thanks.”

“My name’s James. I was just tryin’ to be helpful. Who are you anyway?”

“Thanks again, but this cargo’s a burden I must bear alone,” and she walked past him.

“What did you say your name was?”

She stepped on the first step, turned to him and said, "I didn't," walked into the house, and shut the door firmly. The room's darkness made the figures she saw seem like silhouettes. Her eyes quickly adjusted, and she recognized the general. "I have the cargo you requested from my father in these bags."

Billy came forward to take the bags, but she turned away from him. The general said to her, "Jasmine, I'd trust that man with my life. Billy's my personal valet. He's been with me for years."

Billy put his hands forward to take the saddlebags. Jasmine handed them to him. His eyes widened with surprise at their weight. "Merciful heavens, Mr. George, these sho' is heavy."

Jasmine said to him sternly, "Billy, guard those with your very life."

He looked at her puzzled and then to the general who said, "Do as she says and don't mention to anyone about this matter."

"Yez sir," he said. "You can count on ole Billy."

He exited the room with the heavy bags and quickly returned with a plate of food and a tankard of beer with a frothy head. Billy sat them on the secretary desk, backed away, and said, "This is fo you, missy. Please, sit down. Eat up."

Jasmine said, "Sir, I feel awkward taking your desk."

The general smiled. "Well, Jasmine, your Uncle George wishes you to, and he won't take no for an answer."

"Very well," she said, sat down at the secretary, and began to eat heartily at the beans, potatoes, and salt pork.

George took the other chair and said to his wife, “Please sit down, Martha,” which she did. He said to Billy, “Get me a chair from the other room.”

“Yez sir,” he said and got a wooden chair for the general who sat in it. Billy stood at attention.

“This some good grub here,” Jasmine said. “Ain’t had a hot meal in days.”

“Thank ya,” Billy said.

George Washington said, “Billy’s quite a wizard when it comes to making ordinary vittles seem like a banquet.”

“He certainly is,” Lady Washington said. “His mother was a cook at a neighboring plantation. He picked it up at her apron strings. He’d be running the kitchen at Mt. Vernon for me if he wasn’t my husband’s own servant. I’ve never heard a complaint about his cooking.”

"Thank ya, ma’am. Yous sure does know how to make a compliment. Thank ya,” Billy said.

Jasmine said, “I agree with Lady Washington and His Excellency.”

A broad smile filled Billy’s face.

“George,” Martha said. “You have me curious about what you said about our guest. I can hear the gears turning in your head.”

Jasmine’s eyes moved from her plate to Lady Washington and then to General Washington. She wiped her mouth with her shirt sleeve and waited for him to answer.

The general said, “We have a unique opportunity. Before us stands a person I've watched grow up and her appearance today was a great and welcome surprise. Years ago, I gave her father a great favor, and he's returned it tenfold. He was my trusted courier, aide, and helper when I served the Virginia governor protecting the frontier from Fort Cumberland. He faced formidable odds and enemy forces, but he never let me down. And he's trusted his daughter to bring this special cargo to me which she's done successfully. Jasmine, if you're willing, I'm thinking of a special position for you as my agent."

"Your agent?" Jasmine asked. "I think I need to know more. I think Paw was expecting me to come back soon."

"I can get word to your father," the general said. "It won't be easy considering Old Man Winter has arrived. I would like you to overwinter with us. I need someone I can trust to carry out my orders and slip around our camp and the enemy's positions and attract little if any notice."

"And you think I'm that person?" Jasmine said. "Why?"

"Jasmine," the general said, "I know you're a fearless person. Your father told me once of how you single-handed killed the bandit when you were but twelve." Lady Washington drew in a short breath. The general continued, "You made it here successfully, and I know you can blend in. You might call it hiding in plain sight. All of us here took you to be a lad. You're correct in saying a man can go and do things a woman cannot, but it's also true a woman can do things a man cannot. I believe with my wife's help and proper clothing, you could also pass for a lass if and when needed."

"I hate dresses," Jasmine said.

Lady Washington touched her chin. "George, I believe you've come up with a great and wonderful idea. My mind is running wild about the possibilities."

"Mine too, Martha," the general said. "Jasmine, would you consider my idea?"

"I think it's a good idea, too, Missy Jasmine," Billy said. "Master George has thunk up some bodacious ideas to keepin' this war for independence goin' wif all the odds agin us."

"I hope you're right, Billy," the general said. "What started out so well with the British leaving Boston, has now turned around. If God hadn't clouded British Commander Howe's judgment and sent a morning fog over the bay, we'd have been soundly defeated out on Long Island. Howe had our army in a corner, and we managed to slip away. The rebellion and the fight for freedom would have ended right then and there. Now we're low on supplies and have to second-guess our enemies every next move. He has the advantage on land with more troops, better trained and supplied, plus he has those dreaded German mercenaries. The seas are the King's with his navy, but this land is huge, bigger than he is, so perhaps we can use what we do have to our advantage. I believe until we're stronger, we must bite at our enemy's heels, make him angry, and then run away and do it over and over again until he's worn out or exhausted from his victories. Perhaps we can find an ally or two in some old foe of the British, maybe the French or even the Spanish. How they would love to bloody King George's nose."

Jasmine assessed the General with her eyes, not the eyes of a child as he could remember her, but as the young warrior, she saw herself to be now. "Sir," she said, "if you can pull that off, our necks will be free of John Bull's yoke. I want to throw my hat in the ring, and yes, I'm willing to help in any way I can. Tell my father I'm staying here. I'm of age and can make my own decisions."

"Splendid," the general said. "I have some bold ideas, and I need every man and woman, I can muster for what I've planned before the militiamen's enlistments are up. Perhaps some can be persuaded to stay on. The cargo should help us with that. As for you, Jasmine, continue to present yourself as a young man, a Mr. Phares, Mr. Jasper Phares. Is that agreeable with you?"

A coy grin came to her face. "It is and very clever of you. Jasper Phares, it shall be, I like that."

He continued, "You will answer to me and me alone. You'll be my personal agent. I may even ask your opinion on some of those audacious ideas I have. Would you like to hear one?"

"Yes sir, I would," she said.

He went around the secretary desk and whispered something in her ear. Her eyes widened slightly. "Really?" she said.

"Yes," he said, "there's more." He whispered some more in her ear, and her eyes grew wider.

"General Washington," she said, "you're sly like a fox and have the courage of a badger."

He said, "I have a council of war meeting with my officers on this matter, and I want you to be there. I'll introduce you as my new agent who has come at my request from the western frontier. It will be short, just enough to let them know you are one of us, and I trust you, and they are to do the same. Is that clear, Mr. Phares?"

"Yes, sir. It is. When will this council meet?"

"Tomorrow after the men have their breakfast."

A stir went through the others in the room. Something big was in the air. They looked at the general's face, which had a stern and far-off look. His mind was set. The course was laid. What was it he could see in his distant stare?

***

The Next Morning

"Then it's settled. We move forward with the plan," General Washington said.

General Ewing spoke, "While I still have my reservations on this, I agree. Something must be done against the bloody British and their hired Hessians. I hope that Nature and Nature's God smiles on this bold endeavor."

"I'm in agreement with General Ewing," Colonel Cadwalader said. "If we can pull this off, it could knock them down for some time. My opinion is they will have their guard down with the weather being like this and it being Christmas time."

Others at the war council nodded. Jasmine observed the men's faces for signs of deception but saw none, just looks of reservations and doubts. It was a bold plan, maybe even brash and foolhardy, but it could work. She was a little surprised at how readily she was accepted into the group as Mr. Jasper Phares. The good word General Washington gave to the men about her had done the trick. Clearly, the men held him in high standing, and this group treated his word as gospel.

"We proceed with the plan," General Washington said. "Begin all needed preparations for this immediately, and nothing's to be said to the troops about our destination or the exact date. I know our adversary has spies about, and loose lips could sink this operation before we even attack."

The men agreed and slowly left the room to begin the implementation of the plan. At last, when all had gone except Billy and Jasmine, the general sat down and sighed. A far-off look came again to his eyes.

"General, sir, I think it went well," Billy said.

His eyes focused on his servant, "Better than I expected. There's still much that can go wrong and much to do, but we must do something. Timing is everything and the time is now or never. We must strike when they think they have us beaten or all could be lost." He looked at Jasmine and asked, "So what do you think, Mr. Phares?"

"I listened to all that was said. It is a truly bold plan, but the devil's in the details. I believe it can be done. It won't be easy, and I doubt if all will go as planned, but yes, I believe it can be done."

"Good," General Washington said. "And now I have a special assignment for you, Jasmine."

Jasmine looked at him knowingly. "Does it involve wearing a dress?"

General Washington smiled. "It does, and I know I can count on you to carry it out. Soon I need the ears of the British to have some information, information that will turn out to be slightly off but believable."

"You can count me in, General," she said. "Sometimes, a lass can be a truthful deceiver."

The general smiled again. He knew he had found the right person to do the job.

***

The next day Jasmine, dressed as a servant woman, went to the trading post in the small town. The owner was a man who claimed to be a Patriot but was a known Tory sympathizer. Her instructions were to purchase a quantity of bread for the troops. The owner casually noted she was new to him, and she told him she was at the Patriot's camp and was doing her job to see the men had provisions. He flirted with her as he got her order. This annoyed her, but she tried not to show it. Jasmine fingered the long knife hidden in her dress, wanting so much to use it dramatically to let him know his advances were less than welcome, but she resisted the strong urge. This would ruin the plan. When he turned away, she carefully dropped a handkerchief to the floor. In it was a note signed by General Washington directing General Ewing and Colonel Cadwalader to wait for orders on offensive actions until after the first of the new year. It said they were to remain in place and see to the needs of the men at present and have them ready for actions planned at that time.

All went well. The owner gave her more bread than she asked for. She did not put a knife to his throat as she wanted, and through a window, she saw him find the dropped note. The general knew the letter would then be carried to Hessian forces by Tory spies. His spies got word back to him that the Hessian guard who had been on full alert had dropped back to regular watches and were preparing for a Christmas Day celebration with much imbibing.

As a ruse, Militia Commander Griffin, on December 22, engaged the enemy at Iron Works Hill. This too went well. Hessian forces took the bait and traveled south away from Trenton, one of Washington's possible targets, to Bordentown and waited there for an enemy attack that never happened. As planned, this would put them too far away to return to Trenton's aid. This information was relayed to General Washington. The parts of the puzzle were falling into place. Trenton was now a more desirable target for attack than his original choice of Mount Holly. He informed his staff of his decision on December 23. They would attack Trenton before dawn on December 26.

There would need to be crossings of the Delaware River at three different places into the New Jersey countryside for a three-pronged attack on the Hessian garrison in Trenton. General Washington had seen months earlier that all available boats were on his side of the river, not the other. The Hessians and British were unable to attack as his army regrouped and planned.

On December 24, boats were brought down the river and hidden near Taylor Island. Christmas Day found the river filled with ice flows. If the river froze over, the enemy would soon not need boats to cross and attack. The weather grew worse and worse all Christmas night. Conditions went from miserable to horrible, but it was now or never. General Washington gave the order to proceed. "Death or Victory" was the password.

Throughout the night, a wind like a hurricane blew sleet and snow. Seamen used ferries and Durham boats to carry men, horses, artillery, and ammunition across the ice-filled river. General Washington was on the first boat, and he watched impatiently as his careful plan grew further and further behind schedule. At three AM, the last boat crossed, and it carried Jasmine Phares, who the general had ordered to remain and wait for news on the other crossings.

She saw him anxiously waiting and went directly to him. "Mr. Phares," he asked as his staff crowded around. "What news of the other crossings?"

She shook her head. "Not good, sir. It's not confirmed, but the early word is neither was successful. We could be the only troops to make it across to the eastern side of the river."

A lot of frustration and anger came to his face. "What do we do, sir?" said one of the senior staff.

"I need a moment to think and reflect," the general said. "We're so far behind one more moment will not make any difference. He walked off about one hundred feet. No one followed him. They could see him kneel in the snow, and he bowed his head in prayer. Minutes passed as the staff waited. General Washington arose and began to walk back. As he got close, a man asked, "What do we do, general? What do we do?"

He stopped in front of the men. Fire from the torches lit his face. He seemed to be looking right through them. "We go on. Death or Victory."

The men repeated his words. "Death or Victory."

Chapter 14

"I'm freezin' me balls off," someone uttered among the infantrymen as they marched. Jasmine laughed to herself. If she had any stones to freeze, they'd be like ice also. If only they knew. The wind continued to howl as Washington's army ground on toward the Hessian camp in Trenton. His informants in New Jersey had provided him with the enemy strength, around 1400 men total. He had 2400 at his command and had split them into two groups upon reaching the hamlet of Birmingham, one under his leadership and the other under General Greene, for a two-point plan of attack. Local civilian patriots had led them down the twisting and confusing roads. Many men lacked shoes and wore rags wrapped around their feet. Blood on the ground and snow showed the paths they had trod. General Washington rode back and forth, encouraging the men to continue on as swiftly as they could. Already, the first hint of dawn was showing on the eastern horizon. They marched on toward the small, unwalled town of Trenton, consisting of only two main streets and about 100 homes.

Hessian Commander Rall slept little that night. It was Christmas. What was he doing so far from home in this God-forsaken frozen wilderness? After another swig of hard cider, he wiped his mouth with his sleeve. How he wished for a good German beer on this miserable night. How could he have known 36 years ago when he became a soldier, he would end up like this? His own commander despised him, and his troops certainly did not admire him. They felt him too soft and not ruthless enough in spite of the many battles he had been in. “He’s lazy, loves life too much, and cares little about us,” were comments he’d overheard from the soldiers under his command. He ignored requests for building fortifications around the camp. They didn’t need them and wouldn’t be around that long to bother.

Talk was of attacking the rebels once the river froze and ending this rebellion once and for all. Perhaps then he could return to Germany and live out his remaining days peacefully. That was a pleasant thought. Privately, he laughed at the idea of an attack from Washington's ragtag troops, but in letters to his superiors, he asked for reinforcements that never came. He knew about covering his backside if something did go wrong.

Perhaps tonight, his troops would think more highly of him. He would overlook the men’s imbibing and send out very minimum patrols. Only mad dogs would be out on a night like this, and it was Christmas Day. What kind of a man would seriously consider crossing an ice-filled river in a blizzard at night on this Holy Day? Such thought was lunacy. Still, he’d been warned of an attack. There had been one by raiders, but it was small and quickly repulsed. The enemy had little appetite for battle and fled in disarray after a few shots were fired. That was all that had happened and would happen. Now they could relax again. He drifted back off to sleep in his chair.

The sun was over the horizon when the Patriots reached the outskirts of Trenton. Hessian soldiers spotted them and fired. General Washington led the charge on the outpost, and the enemy was soon in retreat after suffering minor casualties. They regrouped on a hill and met the American forces head-on before again retreating to the town. General Washington ordered men to block the road to Princeton, the apparent escape route. The battle moved to the village where Hessians sniped from windows. Commander Rall awoke, and he hastily ordered defensive measures.

American artillery was brought up and pounded Hessian positions. Again they fell back and were met by other Hessians soldiers coming to battle. Guns blazed in the streets of the town. The second group of American militia entered the fight as Patriot artillery continued to tear into enemy positions. The Hessians retreated again after an American bayonet charge. General Washington shouted orders as he rode back and forth among his men. Billy and Mr. Phares joined in and fired volley after volley at the Hessians, many who had just awakened from sleep and were only half-dressed.

Rall rallied his troops, and they prepared for a counter-attack. "Forward," he yelled. “Advance. Advance.” They began to move to the sounds of their brigade band’s flutes, drums, and bugles, encouraging them on. From his position on a hillside, General Washington saw this and ordered his men to meet the charge. The Hessians found themselves attacked from three directions. Town's people began firing from their homes at their unwanted Hessian "guests." A struggle for a cannon broke out, but the rebels prevailed, and the battle turned into a rout after Hessian Commander Rall was seriously wounded. Seeing this from the hill, General Washington yelled to his men, “March on, my good fellows, after me,” as he led the charge down to town. His forces pursued the Hessians to an orchard where they were soon surrounded. They readily agreed to terms for surrender.

Another separate regiment of Hessians tried to break through Patriot lines, but couldn’t and were surrounded. They, too, choose to surrender. The battle was quickly over with a decisive victory for the rebels. Twenty-two Hessians would die, including Commander Rall, who expired later that same day. Eighty-three were wounded, and close to nine hundred men were taken prisoner. American losses were minimal. Two died from exposure, and five others were injured, one very seriously. George Washington's personal physician and friend would treat him. The injured man's name was James Monroe, and he did recover with time. Men whose names would become famous were also with General Washington that fateful night, names like James Madison, John Marshall, and even rivals Alexander Hamilton and Aaron Burr.

All four Hessian colonels died, and another 200 enemy soldiers were captured south of Trenton. Also seized were enemy cannons, 1,000 arms, 40 horses, and much-needed ammunition. With the taking of the Hessian storehouse, the rebels gained desperately needed supplies, many items the Americans needed just as much as horses and weapons, if not more. Among the booty were shoes and boots, bedding and clothing, tons of flour, meats salted and dried, and much ales and liquors. General Washington put Mr. Phares and Billy in charge of the beverages. The troops would be rewarded with these later. The general knew what calamity could result with drunken soldiers from what had happened at Fort Necessity years ago, and he did not want a repeat of that terrible incident.

Word soon reached the general, giving positive confirmation that they were the only American forces to have made it across the Delaware River into New Jersey. His 2,400 men were isolated. Without the additional 2,600 men still on the other side, he could not continue on to attack Princeton and New Brunswick. He chose to retreat back to Pennsylvania with his prisoners and supplies from their storehouse. The men were worn out and needed a safe place to rest.

This small battle stunned the British and galvanized the colonial effort. It provided a vital psychological advantage for the Americans. Re-enlistments would increase. Congress would provide much-needed money for supplies and troop pay, which always seemed to be in arrears. An army on the brink of collapse had turned the tide of the war.

Jasmine, aka Mr. Jasper Phares, stayed with General Washington as his agent for the rest of the war until Cornwallis surrendered at Yorktown, Virginia. Jasmine was a welcome companion and confidant to Lady Washington while she overwintered with her husband. The young woman, Jasmine, often talked with Billy and learned much about the lives of slaves. Never before had she known one as a person. Previously, she had only seen them from a distance working the fields like beasts of burden, and this experience with Billy affected her deeply.

Both Jasmine and Billy had many adventures during the war while they served General Washington and the patriot cause. Tales and stories were told about them that became myths and legends. Jasmine went on to lead an exciting and full life and became the only woman ever entrusted with the secret of Braddock's Gold, but all of these stories for both of them must remain for telling at another time.

Chapter 15

Monday morning, one week later, 1998

Well, here he was again, sitting in a booth at Linda's Restaurant for lunch. What a week it had been, one he didn't want to live over. Miriah had brought a cold home from school, and now everyone had it, her mom, the baby, and now doggone it, Tom was feeling run down, and his nose was running. Another delivery driver had backed his truck into one of Tom's, and that truck was in the shop. And then the big truck developed a bad miss in the engine. If it went down, he'd be short a truck, and he didn't want to rent a truck from Penske unless he had to. Penske was a good company, but he hated to spend the extra money unless he absolutely had to.

The fish weren't biting in the Potomac River this morning earlier either, and then he nearly ran a big, dark navy blue SUV into a ditch on a turn on narrow Dans Run Road. A deer had been standing a few feet off the road on a hillside. Its eyes seemed to be judging him, and that gave Tom the willies. His eyes were fixed on the deer until a horn blast brought him back to reality. Though the glass on the SUV was heavily tinted, Tom thought a Hispanic man was driving it. Tom's heart pounded almost out of his chest, and he checked to make sure he'd not wet himself. He wondered about the other man.

Padre had called and asked him to meet him here today. The good Padre was running late and had not called. Wonder what he had on his mind? It seemed much was happening in a hurry for Padre, and a lot could go wrong for both of them. And then, what about that call from Rev. O'Reilly? He was the pastor of the Berean Independence Baptist Church over in Fort Ashby. He requested Tom come over today for a talk at 4. Tom didn't know him very well, but they were on friendly terms. Whatever was on, his mind seemed important though he never did get around to saying exactly what it was — only one way to find out.

He sipped at his coffee as he waited. Tom took the liberty to order for them, two specials, sauerkraut, hot dogs, and mashed potatoes. He hoped this would be okay with Padre. His phone began to buzz in his pocket. He pulled it out. The number read 000-000-0000. The man who called himself the Benefactor was calling. How much longer would he wait for Tom to remember where the gold was located? That information remained lost in the PTSD black hole in Tom's head. "Hello," he said.

"Good afternoon, Mr. Kenney," the electronically altered voice said. "I trust all is well with you."

It just went from bad to worst. "I've had better days, but I'll make it," Tom said.

"Did I catch you at a good time, Mr. Kenney?"

"You seem to know when I'm not busy, but no. Now's not a good time. I have an important appointment, and the party I'm meeting just walked in the front door."

"Very well. I will call back later. It has been a while since we talked. I need an update."

"I thought that was the case. Call back in about two hours, and you should find me available."

"Yes, that should be doable. I will look forward to it."

The phone line went dead just as Padre sat down across from him. “Did I interrupt something important?” he said. “You look like you don’t feel so well. Bad news? Sorry, I'm late. My day off has been hectic so far. What's up?"

Tom said, "I'm not sure I even know where to start. Everyone at the house is sick, and I think I may be coming down with whatever it is. I've two trucks with mechanical problems. I think I may be losing my mind, and the person who calls himself my Benefactor was just on the phone.”

Padre whistled through his teeth. “Um-hmm, sounds like you’ve had better days. I had an interesting day so far also. Want to hear about it?”

“Sure, if it’ll cheer me up. Let’s hear it.”

“Well, you know how the county is trying to be sensitive to the needs of the indigent as best they can?”

“Go on.”

"I got a call from the undertaker the county has contracted to bury homeless people. He wanted me to say a few words for a man who had died, and no one claimed the body. He was to be the first person interred in the new Potter’s Field the county opened.”

"Yeah, I think I heard they needed a new spot for that. Been called a few times myself to do services for people like that. Not pleasant, but it doesn't seem right for no one to be there at the sendoff."

“I heartily agree. I got the directions, but as you know, I’m still not too familiar with all the back roads in the county.”

“Yeah, and some of those roads ain’t even marked.”

“I was supposed to be there at 9:30, but I was an hour and a half late when I finally found the site really in the middle of nowhere. The hearse and undertaker had already left. I saw a pile of dirt with men in work clothes sitting on it, taking a break and eating sandwiches. I walked over and saw the hole with the vault already in place. I felt really, really bad about being so late and proceeded to preach an impassioned and lengthy sermon. The guys got up and were getting into the mood, yelling ‘Glory’ and ‘Hallelujah.’ It was something. I finished up and was going to leave when one of the workmen came up to me with tears in his eyes and said, ‘I've been putting in septic tanks for 20 years, and I ain’t never seen nothin’ like this.’”

Tom's mouth dropped open, and then he smiled and laughed. "Padre, you always seem to know what I need. I didn't see that coming, and it was hilarious."

“Yup, the Good Book does say a merry heart does a body good.”

"Good Book's full of great truths and wisdom."

“Very true. Tom, I have to ask you this? Have you been keepin’ your eye on Him, or have you been letting other things have your attention? I don't say this as a put-down, but because I've done it myself."

Tom lowered his eyes. “It’s like you say. Seems like all these little burdens are weighing me down. I tend to forget we can cast all our cares on His broad shoulders.”

“Me too. Think if God thought it important, He’d repeat it several times?”

"Yeah, I do."

“How ‘bout if He said it six times?”

“Then I’d say He was trying to get our attention like a brick to the head.”

“He said six times that Caleb followed Him wholly. I think He was trying to drive home an important point.”

“You think? Six times?”

“Yup. Six times. You know I was feeling pretty low as of lately. That thought has helped me. The secret is no secret. We need to keep our eyes on Him at all times and not get distracted."

“Tell me about it.”

At that time, Debbie showed up with their meals. "Here you go, guys. Enjoy." She left and went back to the kitchen.

Padre looked at the food in front of him. “What’s this?”

“Soul food.”

“Soul food? This doesn’t look like any soul food I’ve ever seen.”

“Well, it’s mountain soul food. You know, comfort food in the Appalachians.”

"Well, okay. I'll try it. Guess I'm going to be living in the hills for some time. When in Rome… The Pittsburgh Police Department accepted my application. Now all I have to do is pass the training. It won’t be easy, but with my background as an MP in the service, I should have a leg up.”

Between bites of food, the men talked. “Pittsburgh, now that’s a town with great ethnic food of many varieties,” Tom said. “Ever had a pepperoni roll?”

“Can’t say I have. This is pretty good.”

"I know that's why I ordered it for you. You're in for some gastric delights in the days ahead. Now FYI, a pepperoni roll's a little white loaf roll kinda doughy chuck full of pepperoni slices or pieces depending on who made it."

"Sounds like a rolled-up pizza slice."

"Yes and no. More like a hot dog bun loaded with pepperoni."

"Okay, sounds good."

"Sometimes the wife gets some of those hoagie rolls from Caporale's Bakery in Cumberland and makes something similar only better. She toasts them slightly and then covers them with her special concoction made of tomato sauce, pepperoni, sweet peppers, and cheeses. It's the closest thing you can make to a Westover Hoagie. One of the locals, his name was Bob White, turned us on to them while Sarah and me were going to West Virginia University in Morgantown. Everyone called him Quail for obvious reasons."

"Obvious," Padre repeated.

Tom said, "You have to make them yourself now. Owners sold the place, and it's a run of the mill sports bar like you find everywhere. Oohhh, they were good. You'd think you died and went to heaven."

"Mmm, mmm. That does sound like angel food." He stopped and looked at Tom.

"What?" Tom asked.

"Could we stop talking about food and eat what's here? I may starve to death while talking about a banquet and having one right in front of me uneaten."

"Okay, I know you didn't ask me here so soon to discuss culinary delicacies. I'll shut up, and you get to the point when we're done."

“Deal,” Padre said.

The two men said nothing more as they attacked the food. Debbie came with coffee. They pointed to their cups. She filled them up and left. No longer talking, the men wolfed the meal.

“That was a welcome surprise. The longer I live, the more I’m willing to try new things,” Padre said.

“Try it with kielbasa sometime. A Polish fellow turned me on to that. Hey, have you ever tried fry bread?”

“Don’t even know what it is.”

"It's little more than flour and lard-fried. It's a Navajo thing. Sarah, my first wife, loved it, but it wasn't for me. I think it's one of those things you have to acquire a taste for."

"Doesn't sound like something I'd like, but then I like pickled pig feet. My uncles would give them to us as we traveled to the ball games."

Tom said, “I’ve tried them. I can take them or leave them.” He stopped. “Ever tried scrapple?”

“Can’t say I have. Is it like chitlins?”

“It’s made with some of the same stuff, only much better.”

“I would certainly hope so.”

Tom said, “Okay, enough about food. What was it you wanted to chat with me about today?”

Padre, aka Father Frank, smiled, "Tom, my friend, I've got a huge favor to ask."

“Padre, you know if there’s any way possible for me to do it, I will, so don’t keep me in suspense. What is it?”

Chapter 16

Padre said, "I'd like you to marry Stacy and me on Monday, two weeks from now."

“Two weeks? That’s not much notice.”

"I know. Things are happening like popcorn popping in my life now. I got accepted by the Pittsburgh Police Department, and they want me ASAP, if not sooner. I'm turning my resignation in to the Bishop today. This Sunday will be my last day doing my official duties. I don't know how long he'll give me to be out. Stacy has that Monday off, and my twin brother Freddie said he’d take the day off and be my best man. It's not going to be elaborate. We'd like you to do it at the overlook at Cooper’s Rock State Forest this side of Morgantown at 10 o’clock.”

“What if it rains?”

“We’ll do it in one of the pavilions.”

“And the reception?”

“Everyone who shows up is invited to Ruby and Ketchy's at Cheat Lake. Their back room was open. We meet there, order off the menu, have a good time, and it's all on me."

Tom said, “Sounds like you’ve got this thought out. What if I’m busy?”

“Would you check your schedule, please?”

Tom pulled his planner from his hip pocket and opened it. He looked up at Padre. “You’re in luck.”

“I thought I might be that being the usual day you try to take off after your sermon on Sunday.”

“Days off have been few lately, but you do what you got to do. You can count on me.”

Padre said, “Your wife and kids are all invited. I don’t think there’ll be too many people. She doesn’t have very many relatives, and I'm not going to announce it to my church. Not sure how they will react to me quitting and then turning around and getting married."

“I see your point. It’ll work out. I’m sure the Catholics have a grapevine, word will get out, and those interested will show.”

“I was thinking the same thing. Glad that’s working out. I hope it does for you. Still, have that feeling like it's about to hit the fan?"

Tom said, “I do. Just as you were driving up, I got a call from him, the guy who calls himself the Benefactor. It’s crazy, but I’ve got this gut feeling I’ve met him somewhere before. And I haven’t been able to shake the sensation that there’s a hurricane coming. Things are about to change big time for me.”

“I’ve just been through that, Tom. All I can say is to hang in there and trust your gut feeling. It’s there for a reason. In ways we can’t even imagine, God’s at work in our lives. Maybe the reason He’s taking you through deep waters is your enemies can’t swim.

Just outside of my window at the church, I had a flower come up in a crack in the sidewalk. What an environment, but in spite of this hostile place, it took root and flourished. I couldn't figure how it was thriving when the grass was dying from the lack of rain until I noticed water from the air conditioner in the window was draining down the crack, and the plant flourished and produced a beautiful flower. I think God sent that flower for me, and I think He meant for me to pass that on to you and anyone else who needed it."

"We'll see. My Benefactor is calling back in an hour or so, and I'm not sure he'll be impressed with your sermon."

"He may not, but no matter how dark the night or strong the storm, our Lord is still more powerful and isn't in a panic. God's always good and faithful. Old Job is a great example. After his troubles hit him big time, he said, 'Shall we accept good from God, but not troubles?' I know the pain of our circumstances can seem overwhelming, been there, but He's always present to help us through the hard times. Remember when Peter walked on water at the Sea of Galilee? He was doing good till he took his eyes off Jesus and looked at the waves."

"Yes, I know. There's another lesson there. Old Pete walked and talked with the Lord for several years, and he still messed up on a regular basis."

"Very true," Padre said. "And through it all, Jesus was with him."

"I think I can relate to Peter. I'm glad the Good Book tells us about both the failings and successes of the people recorded there."

"Me too." There was a brief silence between them as they reflected on the great truths they had just shared. "Say, you do know you're paying today. Last time, I paid. You'd conveniently forgotten your wallet."

"Yeah, I remember. I've got cash today."

"Good, and Tom, one last thing. No gift from you. You doing the wedding will be your gift. How does that sound?"

"Sounds good."

The two men got up to leave. Tom dropped a twenty on the table, and they headed to the front door. Debbie was at the cash register. Her eyes met Tom's. He said, "I left a twenty on the table. That should take care of it, right?"

"More than enough," she said.

"Consider the extra your tip."

She smiled, "Thanks, Tom. Say hello to the wife for me. I haven't seen much of her lately."

"I will. She's been pretty busy with the new baby. Both of them have been sick with colds."

"Yeah, seems like half the people who come in here have the sniffles or worst."

"See ya, Debbie."

She nodded, "Till next time."

"You bet."

Tom walked outside through the double doors. Padre was waiting. Tom looked around. "What are you looking for?" Padre said. "Are you expecting someone?"

"Well, I already know this Benefactor fellow seems to know where I am even before I do, but in all honesty, I was looking for a deer. I still can't shake the feeling those eyes left."

“You remember what we talked about. God’s in control, and we needn't panic."

“I gotcha Padre. Easier said than done.”

“I’ll be praying for you, Tom.”

“Do that and the females in my life.”

“How could I forget them? See ya later.”

"Yeah, later. Call me if you need to make any changes to the wedding or anything else."

“Wilco, over and out. “

They walked to their cars, got in, and drove off. Tom followed Padre on Route 28. He took a right at his house and pulled the car up to the back of the house. He got out, walked to the house, and went in. Joann was sitting at the table. She had a look of concern on her face. Tom’s face fell when he saw her. “What’s wrong?” he said.

“Dark Cloud called. He said it’s imperative. Call him back around six real-time, not Indian time, at the chapter house.”

Dark Cloud. He hadn’t heard from him in several years. What could he want now that was so important?

Chapter 17

Dark Cloud was the father of his first wife, Sarah. Actually, he was her uncle, but he'd raised her as his own after the death of her mother. Tom had met her brother, Chris, in Vietnam. He'd always said Tom should meet his sister. Tom thought it idle talk among soldiers sharing in that hellhole called war to keep their sanity. If Chris hadn't taken that bullet, Tom would be where Chris was now, dead. If not for the dying promise Tom had given him to tell his father how he died with honor in battle, he would have never met Sarah. He'd tried to avoid fulfilling his promise, but happenings and events saw he did. And what a difference it had made in his life.

Dark Cloud. What could he want? Tom's mind raced at the possibilities, but he knew the answer would have to wait until tonight. There was much to do before that time.

"So, he didn't say much about what he wanted?" Tom asked.

"No, he made some small talk, asked how we were doing, but whatever was on his mind, he meant for your ears only. He did say you'd understand," Joann said.

"Could be a number of things or something completely different. I'll have to wait till tonight when I call him. Six his time, real-time, not Indian time and at the Navajo chapter house?"

“Yes, the one in Lukachukai. He said you know the number. What do you think he wants?”

“I don’t know, but it must be important.” Tom took a deep breath. “It’s been an interesting day so far and gonna get more interesting before I hit the hay tonight. First, my nose is runnin', and I think you and the baby are sharing your colds with me. You know about the problems at work. The fish weren't biting, and I nearly got in a wreck on Dans Run Road, and it would've been my fault. I was distracted by something. Then the meeting with Padre. He wants me to marry him and Stacy two Mondays from now at Cooper’s Rock, and I got a call from the Benefactor.”

“Sounds like you’ve had some day so far.”

“You don’t know the half of it. I put the Benefactor off for about an hour. He should be calling soon. After that, I've got an appointment with Rev. O’Reilly at four o’clock, and he was vague about what he wanted. And now Dark Cloud pops up after a long hiatus. I know everything happens for a reason, but when it rains, it pours.”

"Seems that way. Do you want anything? Oh, Doug said he had everything under control with our bottled water business. Said it felt like herding cats, but he had them all corralled for now."

“That’s a bit of good news I can appreciate. Want something? Do we have any apples?”

She said, “Got a bag of Galas from Wayne’s Grocery when I was shopping the other day. And something special for you, scrapple.”

Tom smiled, “Thanks, I know you can’t stand the stuff, but I love it. Add a little butter and some maple syrup, and there's nothin' better."

"Tom, I don't think I'll ever get used to your country ways. Those stories you tell of eating tongue, kidneys, and every part of the offal, even cow brains turn my stomach."

"I think you'd like it if you would try it. Times were lean growing up, and no part of the animal we slaughtered on the farm went to waste. If you think those things are gross, you don't even want to know about what I saw people eating while in Vietnam."

"Please, no. The very idea of this all turns my stomach, Tom. And don't get any ideas of serving me mystery meat. You know what happened last time."

How well he remembered. She liked it pretty good until he told her it was possum and raccoon meat. Then it all came back up. She was not a happy camper and had a burr under her saddle for a week. "Okay Joann, no more mystery meat." If he ever did want to do it again, which was unlikely, he wasn't going to tell her what it was. What she didn't know wouldn't hurt her or get him in the dog house. He said, "I'll grab some apples, some for me and some for Nacho."

"Good thinking. We'd never hear the end of his braying if you forgot him. Better get some treats for Tripod. He's sure to show up too."

"I will." Tom got some apples from the refrigerator and dog treats from a cabinet drawer and went outside. The sun would soon be going behind Knobley Mountain. He walked to the fenced-in pasture around the barn. Nacho heard him coming, came out of the barn, and walked to Tom. The Jerusalem donkey made some funny sounds in his throat that almost sounded like he was donkey purring. "Look what I've got for you, ole boy?" Tom slipped an apple out of his pocket and gave it to Nacho. He mouthed it, and with a few crunches, it was gone. He looked for more. Tom gave him a second, and it quickly disappeared too. Nacho looked like he was expecting another. "No, Nacho. The last one's for me, but I promise you can have the core." He seemed to understand. Tom sat down on a nearby stone wall.

He took a bite of the apple, juicy and sweet. Something rubbed against his back. It startled him. “Tripod! You sure know how to make an entrance. You like to scared me out of a year’s growth.” The dog snorted as only he could. Tom handed him a treat and petted his head. As Tom ate the apple, he continued to feed the dog treats until they were all gone. Tripod looked for more. “That’s all of them, no more.” Tom showed Tripod his empty bag.

The dog seemed a little disappointed. He snuggled against Tom, lay down, and shut his eyes. Tom looked at the content three-legged dog. Yes, there was a lesson lying next to him. Happy to be alive and dealing with unfortunate circumstances life had thrown at him. Today, Tom was listening.

Nacho strained his neck over the fence. He had his mouth open, waiting. Tom stood up and stuck the apple core in the open mouth. Just then, his phone rang, 000-000-0000, the Benefactor was calling. “Hello? Benefactor, how are you?”

“Good, and you?

"Getting by." Tom smiled. "I just shoved an apple core in my ass." There was no response, and then it dawned on Tom what he had said. “Maybe I need to rephrase that last statement. I fed my hungry donkey the core from an apple I’d just eaten.”

“You had me worried, Mr. Kenney. There are some strange and kinky people in this world, but I never took you to be one. I am glad you have not disappointed me.”

“Sorry about that. Glad I could clarify it properly.”

"Perfectly all right. I have been watching anyway. Your little three-legged dog gave you quite a fright and now the business with your Jerusalem donkey. Mr. Kenney, you do surprise me at times."

Tom said, "So you are watching me right now?"

"Yes. Does that surprise you?"

"No, but it's kind of unnerving. You're not watching me in my house, are you?"

"No Mr. Kenney, I am not. You may not understand the rules I live by, but no, even I have places I will not go. Your home's privacy is intact and will remain so. We have an agreement. When you remember where the gold is, you tell me, and I leave you alone. No harm will come to you or your family."

"And I can trust you on that?

"Mr. Kenney, you are an honorable and honest man. There are so few like that in this world. I will treat you the same. For what it is worth, you have my word on it. I will keep my part of the bargain as long as you keep yours. Fair enough?"

"Guess I'll have to trust you on that."

"And I, you."

"One more question for you."

"Okay. What is it?"

"Why are you called the Benefactor?"

"Mr. Kenney, I am known by many names. The less you know, the better for you."

“Benefactor, there is something I need to tell you. I had a dream the other night. In it, I told you I wanted this to be over.”

“I do too.”

“Funny, but you said that in my dream too.”

“That is interesting. Tell me more.”

“I pulled out a gun and emptied the clip in you. You didn’t die, but were resurrected into a Phoenix and flew away. I turned, and it was behind me. It said, ‘I am Darkness, and I will save you.’”

“A Phoenix, you say, and I mentioned Darkness?

"Most interesting, Mr. Kenney. Perhaps you should see someone who interprets dreams, but I hear they are in short supply.”

“It was pretty weird, but I do want this to be over.”

“As do I.”

Tom said, “So let me guess, you still want to know if I can remember the information that will lead to the whereabouts of the Braddock’s Gold payroll.”

“Yes, you read my mind. I am feeling impatient about this matter today. What do you have new to tell me?”

“Nothing.”

“Nothing?”

“Absolutely nothing. I was hoping something would come to me, some random electron would fire and hit those memory cells, and I would know, but nothing. I've hoped something would jar my memory, but nothing. It’s like it disappeared into a black hole."

“That is very disappointing.” There was silence. “I grow weary and disappointed at the wait.”

"In that, we agree. Giving you that information would get you off my back, and I honestly believe I'd never hear from you again."

“That was the agreement, Mr. Kenney, and I keep my deals. It is good business. I will see you are not harmed. Everyone lives happily ever after.”

“I’ve heard that somewhere before.”

“With me, it is not a fairy tale. As I said, everybody goes away a winner. We each receive what we want."

“You know there’s a far greater treasure than gold and silver, one that thieves can’t steal, and you can never lose.”

“You’ve piqued my interest in many ways, Mr. Kenney. Please continue.”

“As you know, I’m a preacher. I firmly believe that Jesus Christ is the final and only answer to forgiveness of the guilt every member of humanity has. He’s the reason for living, the reason for everything, and when I die, I look forward to seeing my Lord and hearing Him say, “Well done, good and faithful servant. Enter into paradise with Me forever. It’s the greatest treasure and good news ever told to mankind.”

“Mr. Kenney, what could I expect from a preacher but a good sermon? When I grew up, I saw a lot of dead religion. A number of the people I should have been able to look up to as role models were sinful people, and they often wore robes. In you, Mr. Kenney, I see the real genuine article. Your religion is not skin deep but is in your heart and every pore of your body. You talk the talk, and you also walk the walk.”

"It's available for everyone. Jesus said, 'Come unto me, all who are burdened and weighed down. I will give you rest.' Everyone's included in that statement, all of us."

"You know, Mr. Kenney, I like you. You seem like a wonderful man, always caring for others, even those who can and have harmed you, even if your crazy desires come to light in your dreams."

"My Benefactor, it's called forgiveness. I'm to forgive others as the Lord forgave me. I had a debt of sin as big as a mountain, and He paid it all."

"Mr. Kenney, you have no idea how big my mountain is."

"Benefactor, even if your debt is bigger than the Himalayans and Mount Everest, God's love and forgiveness is greater."

The line was silent for a moment. "Mr. Kenney, you have given me much to think about, the divine treasure you tell me about, and the other in gold. I'll consider your words, and you try to think on the earthly treasure I asked you about. Fair enough?"

"Fair enough. When will I hear from you again? I have no way of contacting you."

"You do now. If you remember where the treasure is, you can call the number that came up on your screen. You will reach me. Just make sure it is important. Small talk and disappointments are things I do not tolerate. I do not take disappointment well. Good day, Mr. Kenney. Take care of your dog and your ass. We both need to watch and take care of it."

The line went dead. There was no dial tone for a moment, but as he waited, it did return.

Tom slipped the phone into his pocket. What to do? What to do? He pondered this for a while. He didn't know. Just like a card game, he had to play with the hand he had. Try to be content with things as they were and hope for the best, but what could Rev. O'Reilly want? And Dark Cloud? What indeed? He would soon find out, and he hoped whatever it was wouldn't add to his problems.

Chapter 18

Tom walked back to the house and entered. Joann was fixing some supper. He looked around and wondered what she was cooking. He saw some fresh French bread, and the smell was familiar, though he couldn't place it. "What's you cooking, Jo?"

"I've been told it's called a Westover hoagie. Padre called while you were out. He mentioned how you talked about how great they were, so I'm trying to make them for us. I had all the items necessary, except hoagie rolls, so I'm substituting those with French bread. Sound acceptable?"

"Sounds and smells great. Anything I can do to help out?"

"Wash up and get plates and silverware out. And drinks. I want milk. Get whatever you want from the frig."

"Okay." Tom quickly washed and set the table. He got a Coke from the refrigerator for himself and poured a glass of milk for Joann. "What about Miriah? Is she here?"

"No, she's staying with her cousins tonight. We're here by ourselves. Anything else you want?"

"Some quick lovin' would be fine."

Joann rolled her eyes. “I should have known. Later.”

Tom smiled, “Joann?”

“What?”

“It’s later.”

Joann scrunched up her face, “Much later. Let’s eat this now and see if it’s as good as you remembered. I’ll see about your other needs tonight if I’m not asleep when you get back. I was up and down all night with the baby.”

“I slept well.”

“I know. I can’t understand how a mother can hear a whimper from her child when she's dead asleep, and a man sleeps like a dead man when his child is screaming bloody murder."

“I don’t know either. Guess it must come with the Y chromosome.”

Joann placed the hot open-faced hoagie in front of Tom and then one on her plate. She sat down, took his hand, and he prayed a quick blessing. Tom licked his lips and took a bite. His eyes lit up. “This is really good, Jo. It’s a little different from what I remember, but this is tasty."

Joann took a bite. “Yes, it’s good. Think you’ll be seeing this more often.”

Tom nodded his approval. The hoagies went down the hatch quickly. As they cleaned up and put leftovers into the refrigerator, the new baby began to cry. “Could you take it from here, Tom? The mother can hear the baby crying.”

Tom grimaced. “Sure thing, and I need to get going in the next few minutes if I want to be on time with my meeting with Rev. O’Reilly.”

“Okay, this may take a while. Go ahead and go if I don’t get right back.”

Tom finished the cleanup and washed the dishes and pots in the sink. He looked at his watch and realized he needed to go now. He grabbed a flannel shirt from a coat tree and yelled up the stairs to Joann, "Honey, I'm leaving. Be back whenever the good reverend and me are done. Love you."

“No need to hurry on my part,” came the female voice from upstairs. “I’ll be fine.” A sneeze and then another followed.

Tom shook his head. He muttered to himself, "Yeah, we'll all be just fine except for these colds or flu or whatever it is." He exited the house and hopped in his old Chevy truck. Another year older, a lot more miles and a lot more rust, but the six banger under the hood was still going strong. He drove on a few miles and noticed the state had installed another 100 feet of guardrails. What this road needed was straightened and rebuilt from the ground up. He rounded another blind turn and found a Fort Ashby Volunteer Fire Company man in his gear standing in the road. He held his hand up, commanding Tom to stop. As he slowed, he saw the fire truck down the road with its lights on. Tom recognized the fireman. He rolled the truck window down. “Hey, Bob. What’s going on?”

“Accident, Tom. Not a pretty sight. A truck got sideswiped, the driver lost control, the truck rolled, the driver wasn't wearing a seat belt, and the truck ended up on top of him. Probably would have survived if he was belted up, but that's a moot point now."

“Anybody I would know?”

"Don't think so. Tags were from Pennsylvania. The truck had an advertisement on the bumper from a dealership in Bedford."

“Just the same, we should keep his family in our prayers whoever he was.”

“Amen to that brother. Life’s short, and heaven and hell are forever.”

“Couldn’t have said it better myself.”

At that time, a string of traffic came from around the turn down the road. Bob got out of the way of the oncoming traffic. When it passed, Tom heard a muffled female voice come from Bob’s radio at his side. He picked it up and spoke into it, then he turned to Tom, and directed him to go. The wreck was not pretty. The truck looked like it had rolled several times and rested upside down. Several men were looking under the truck, but no one seemed to have a sense of urgency. Tom drove on around the turn, said a prayer, and continued toward Fort Ashby.

He crossed the bridge over Patterson Creek and saw kids playing baseball in the fields at the county fairgrounds. He caught the town’s only light on green, turned left onto Dans Run Road, passed the Old Fort across from the elementary school, and a mile later, he pulled into the parking lot of the Berean Church. A truck was pulling out. He recognized the man driving it, waved to him, and the man waved back as he left. Only one vehicle remained in the lot, the pastor’s. Whatever Rev. Rory O’Reilly wanted, Tom would soon find out.

Tom saw him sitting in an uncompleted room off to the right. His eyes rose to Tom, and he said, "Come on in. Pardon the construction dust. Gonna be a few more weeks till we get back to the new normal."

"Yeah, I heard about the fire, but I didn't realize it was this bad."

“It was. A lot of damage on the inside you can’t see from the road plus we decided to do some renovations the deacons had been discussing before the fire. We’ve been meeting out back in the Gym building in the meantime.”

"Where are all the workers? I saw their travel trailers over by Dennison Run, but no one seems to be there."

“They took a well-needed mini-vacation. Most will be back next week. A few needed more time, but they’ll all be back in full swing soon.”

“What did you call me over here for today? Your tone seemed like it was important.”

The Reverend’s expression changed. “It is. Very important, and it involves you. I think I have some of Braddock’s Gold lost payroll found right here on church property.”

“You do? How much?”

“A box full.”

“That sounds like a lot.”

“It is. Let me get it.” He rose from his seat and walked to the far side of the church. He moved a partial sheet of drywall and carefully picked up an old and dirty metal box. The only thing that seemed to hold it together was rust. He placed it on a sturdy workman’s table and opened it. Tom’s eyes about bugged out as he looked at the box full of gold coins. “Wow,” he said. He picked one up and looked at it closely. “I think this is the real thing. These look like gold guineas, and that's one of the English Kings named George from the 1700s."

“Yeah,” the Reverend said. “Big wow. I called you for two reasons. Number one: In a small town like this, it’s hard to keep a secret. It’s an open secret that you’re up to your neck in this Braddock’s Gold thing. When I was in the military, we would call your situation a Charlie Foxtrot and sometimes a chaotic fiasco. I knew you’d want to know about this, and possibly you could shed some light on whether this is related to the lost payroll. I think it is.”

Tom said, “I agree. It looks like the real McCoy. What’s number two?”

“Number two: I’ve seen a coin like these before right here in this very church. It showed up in the offering plate some time ago.”

Tom’s eyes widened. “Timmy Miltenberger, who lives a stone’s throw away from here, found some coins like this in the creek and dropped one in the offering plate at the Catholic Church a mile from here the way the crow flies.”

"Well, it wasn't Timmy who dropped it in our plate. It was Dan Phares. He came up to me the following Monday rather sheepish like and finally after hemming and hawing around for what seemed like an eternity, he got it out he had lost his lucky coin, and he thought maybe he had dropped it in the offering. One of the deacons had found it and given it to me for safekeeping. I gave it back to him with instructions to keep it safe as I thought it was precious. He said he would, but you know Dan."

“I do. He’s a strange bird. Harmless. Got a good heart, but naive. I went to school with him. He’s autistic best I can figure out.”

“That’s Dan, all right. And that leads us back to this one fact; all three times, the gold has turned up right here in this small neighborhood.”

Tom said, “Very true, but who or what ties this all together?”

"I'm not sure, but I know you'll figure it out. All this is what I called you over here for today."

Tom thought for a moment. "What are you going to do with the gold?"

"The fewer people who know about this, the better. I've got a place in mind that's safe until we can sort this all out."

"Agreed." Tom seemed preoccupied, lost in thought for a moment. He eyed the Reverend, who was looking at him strangely. "What?"

"You drifted off for a moment. Did something come to you?"

Tom shook his head, "Yes, and no. Seemed like there was something, but it was like staring at a reflection in a mirror in a very dark room. I don't know what it is or was, but maybe it will return cleared up next time."

"I think you're right, Tom. Let's hope this eureka moment comes soon for you."

"And then what?"

"Maybe then we can put this Braddock's Gold matter to bed once and for all."

"I hope you're right. You've no idea the trouble it's caused. I've even been dreaming about how this could end."

"Trust in the Lord and play it by ear. You're welcome to call. I can be a good sounding board if you need one."

"Pastor Rory, I'll keep that in mind. Maybe it will come to me in another dream. Maybe I'll find that lost file in my head. I hope it's soon. I want this to be over." Tom looked at the door.

The reverend said, “Tom, before you leave, can I pray for you?”

“Sure. We should have done that first. We’re going off half-cocked without asking for His help.”

The two men held hands. Reverend O’Reilly began, “All mighty God, Your word says when two or more are gathered, You are there. Lord, hear my prayer. We have a lit stick of dynamite in our hands. We don’t know how long the fuse is, and we’re like blind men. Lord, guide my brother through this dangerous situation and lead him carefully on this slippery path. And Lord, could you do it soon? Our patience is running thin. Amen.”

“Amen to that. Truer words have not been spoken. Thanks for the information. May your prayer be answered soon, very soon. I better go.”

“Like I said Tom, if I can be of any help, just call me.”

“Thanks. Bye.”

“Take care, Tom.”

Tom walked to his car and got in. He swung around the parking lot and stopped at the highway. Across the road and up the hill to the right was the old farmhouse Dan Phares called home. Dan still had his eggs for sale sign out. He wondered how business was. Slightly to the left and about 1500 feet away was the Miltenberger house by Patterson Creek. And directly behind him was the church where the latest gold had turned up. Clues were staring him in the face, but the view was as clear as mud. Oh, how he hoped his lost memories would shake loose.

He turned left on the road heading to Fort Ashby. He still had to talk to Dark Cloud later. What did he want? Tom had a gut feeling more trouble was coming, but what?

Chapter 19

The drive back to his home was uneventful. The wreck had been cleaned up, and nothing showed but a few skid marks and some broken glass that bloody WV State Route 28 had claimed another life. How many more would have to die before the state did something about this death trap?

He pulled into his driveway, went up the slight hill, and saw a strange vehicle with Florida tags parked behind his house. Someone was sitting in it, and the body shape told him it was a man. Cautiously Tom pulled up beside the vehicle. The man looked familiar. He knew him. It was Roger Pyles.

The men got out of their vehicles. Tom said, "Hello, Roger. Long time, no see. What brings you to this neighborhood? Why aren't you in the Sunshine State?

"Good to see you, Tom. Far better than last time when we both almost went to jail. I'm doing pretty good. What am I doing here? I wish it was under better circumstances, but my late wife's father passed, so I'm up here for the funeral. Sad how families only get together for funerals and weddings."

"Yeah, I can relate. My family's the same. How long have you been waiting?'

“Not long. After I disabled your alarm systems, I rapped on the door, but got no answer.”

“My alarm systems?

“The dog and donkey. The latter fussed up a storm that I thought would wake the dead. I gave him an apple, and then we were friends.”

Tom smiled as he thought of his recent fiasco with Nacho and an apple, but he said nothing. "His name’s Nacho, but how did you get past the dog?”

“He growled at me at first. I talked to him a little. What I think converted him to accepting me was he probably smelled my dog on me.”

“You still got K9?’

“Yes I do, and a cat.”

“Never thought of you as a cat person.”

“The cat just showed up and made herself at home. I think someone dumped her off. She was half-starved and terrified. When I first saw her eating the dog’s food, she took off like greased lightning. Took me a long time to get her to trust me, but now we’re buddies. I’ve been cat-lapped many times by her. Once she makes herself at home in my lap, moving her’s a chore. Those claws come out, and you better be careful removing her, or you're gonna get scratched. She's a tortoiseshell and has the personality of Tigger. Bouncy, bouncy, bouncy. I named her Patches.”

“We’ve had one like that when Sarah and me were first married, but we’re down to a dog and a donkey now, no cats or other critters. So you passed the dog test with flying colors?’

"Yup, and after that, I went to the door and knocked. I figured with all the racket those two made, the dead woulda been woke up, but no one answered, so I waited. I was about to give up, but here you are."

"My wife's in there. The baby's been sick, and neither of them are gettin' much sleep. She probably nodded off and was dead to the world. Lucky for you, she was. She may have met you at the door with a 9mm, and she knows how to use it."

Roger said, "Country girl. I should have known. Just like the sticks where I live in Florida, everyone has a gun available or several."

"Why don't you come in and fill me in some more on what you're doing here and also on what you've been up to since I last saw you over a decade ago."

"Sounds good."

"Need something to drink or eat?

"Yeah, I'd appreciate that."

Tom unlocked the door, and the two men went into the kitchen. "Make yourself at home. If you don't mind instant, I can get you a cup of coffee quick and heat up a leftover sandwich."

Tom placed a cup of water in a microwave oven, set the timer, and grabbed a Tupperware container from the refrigerator along with a hot dog bun. He spooned the contents into the split bun on a Corelle plate. A ding told Tom the water was hot. He opened the microwave, took out the water now hot, placed the loaded bun inside, and restarted the microwave. Soon Roger had a cup of coffee and a hot mini hoagie in front of him. "Thanks a million," he said and took a bite. "Hey, this is good. What is it?"

"It's our version of a hoagie we discovered while going to WVU. Call it a Westover hoagie. Pretty simple to make. Cook up some pepperoni, spicy tomato sauce, green peppers. Top it all off with some assorted cheeses and voila; you have a Westover hoagie."

“I’ll remember that. Thanks.” Roger wolfed down the food and wiped his mouth. “I didn’t realize I was so hungry. So tell me, you wanna go first on what you’ve been up to since I last saw you, or should I?”

“You go ahead.”

"Okay, not much to tell. I figured out the case I was working on while you were there. It nearly got me killed, and we stirred up a hornet's nest in Florida involving national security, but justice prevailed even if it was in a roundabout way. I'm still a member of the Canaveral Flats Police Department, still unpaid, and still not sure of what my official title is. On a more positive note, I'm working with local and other law enforcement on solving murders and cold cases. The pay’s nothing to write home about, but I have minimum oversight. They leave me alone for the most part because I get results. And I find evidence they missed and can make it so a jury can understand all the scientific mumbo-jumbo in laymen's terms. The prosecution, defense teams, and judges know me and know if I say it’s so, then it’s the gospel truth. It’s been rewarding.”

“Still drinking?”

“Some, probably more than I should, but I haven’t been arrested for it.”

“I remember the night we almost did.”

“I’d like to forget about it. Bill still uses it as leverage on me. His pulling strings with that deputy was what kept us out of jail.”

Tom said, “Sarah never forgave you for that. She died not too long after. Oh my, did you have her Indian blood stirred up. She threatened to turn your private parts into a nose warmer and a coin purse.”

“I heard about that. Why do you think I stayed away so long? I don’t get back up here very often. I was sorry to hear she’d died.”

“It knocked the wind out of me. I thought I’d never recover, but you have to. You have obligations, and time does help heal the wounds. And how is ole Bill? I’ve not heard from him since then.”

“Bill’s doing fine, still single, still got more girlfriends than the sultan with his harem, and still doing his job. He loves his job as the Chief of Police in Canaveral Flats. He’s still going strong, but his full speed ahead is a little slower than it used to be.”

"Yeah, that sounds like Bill. That's good to hear."

“Any other questions?”

“How long are you going to be in the Cumberland area?”

“About a week or maybe less. Funeral is the day after tomorrow. I want to see some friends, and you never know what'll come up. Other than the funeral, my days are pretty open, making plans as opportunity pops up. So tell me, what’s new with you?”

“As you know, my first wife, Sarah, died in a car crash years ago. Today, out of the blue, her father, a great guy named Dark Cloud, called from out on the Big Navajo Reservation in the Four Corners region. I haven’t heard from him in several years. I missed his call and am calling him back shortly, around six tonight. I don’t know what he wants, but expect it’s important. Our son, Brian, took his own life a year to the day after her death. It was a hellish year.”

Roger said, “We have something in common. We’ve both lost a wife and a son. I didn’t know about your son’s passing, but I do know what it’s like to lose two family members. I wouldn’t wish that on my worst enemy.”

“Very true.” He stopped to catch his breath. “I started the bottled water business I talked to you about while I was in Florida, and it’s going great. My biggest problem is growing pains, which is a great pain to have. My second son, Doug, runs the office, and I act as chief executive plus everything on down to the janitor. It keeps me hoppin'."

"Yeah, you would.”

“Let me tell you, today has been so busy I feel like I've been drinking from a fire hose and the day's not over yet."

“What happened today?”

“For starters, my friend and confidante, a Catholic priest, tells me he wants me to marry him and his girlfriend two Mondays from now.”

“Whoo Nellie, did I get you right? A Catholic priest wants you to marry him? That’s a new one on me.”

“He’s a great guy. Priests are people too. At least, it’s a woman. He’s resigning his position this week and moving on to a new vocation where he thinks he can be of more service to humanity. He’s gonna be a cop in a big city. That’s the nutshell version.”

“The world certainly does need the thin blue line to keep us from descending into anarchy. I hope he does well.”

“I do too.”

Roger said, “So what else?”

“Ever heard of the Braddock’s Gold legend?”

“Can’t say I have. Lots of things around here with that name, Braddock’s Run, Braddock’s Road, Braddock’s Elementary School.”

“All named after English General Braddock of the French and Indian War era. The story goes back to 1755 when his large military payroll consisting of gold coins disappeared somewhere in this area. Today these coins would be worth millions. They were to pay for his nine-month campaign against the French and their Indian allies. Somehow and somewhere, I stumbled across information that can locate the treasure. I can’t remember much about this. I’ve been dealing with PTSD since Vietnam. It causes holes in my memory, and that information went down one of those black holes. There’s been this nemesis who calls on an untraceable phone and speaks through an electronically altered voice. He calls himself the Benefactor. He wants the gold, knows my condition, and wants the gold for himself. This fellow, whoever he is, has got to have big-time connections. He's been watching me like a lurker or stalker. He tells me if I see he gets the treasure, he'll leave my family and me alone. So far, he's done that, and what's really funny, I think he can be trusted to do just that."

“Wow, that’s industrial strength strong.” He rubbed his chin. “You know, gold will make you crazy. I’ve seen it do just that in Florida. There’s Spanish gold, silver, and other treasures all over Florida, most of it along the coast. I’ve investigated some of the crimes associated with this. You say he called you today?”

“Twice. Once at a restaurant a mile toward Cumberland and the other time, while I was feeding Nacho at the fence. He was watching me at the latter place. He said as much.”

“Mission Control, we have a problem. Damn.”

"And I'm a preacher now, so I'd appreciate it if you don't use foul language, especially in my home."

“Sorry,” Roger said. “I’ll try not to let it happen again. Maybe I can help you with this, me being a crime and forensics specialist.”

“I’d appreciate that. I want this to end. I’m tired of looking over my shoulder.”

“I know what you mean. How was the rest of your day?”

"It kept getting crazier as it went along. Another pastor friend wanted to see me at his office. I went, and he showed me an old metal box that was dug up on the church property, and it was full of old gold coins. And furthermore, I know of two other instances where gold coins were found all within a quarter of a mile of the church.”

“That’s an important clue. Everything seems to put the area around the church in a bullseye. Figure out where it leads, and you may very well find the info you need to solve the mystery.”

“I agree. I can feel it in my bones; the answer is there. It’s on the tip of my tongue, and I can't spit it out."

“Give it time. It’ll come.”

“I don’t believe we have much time. I feel like I’m on a volcano getting ready to blow.”

“Where were you when said he was watching you, all the time?

“Up on top of the mountain behind the house and out by the donkey barn. He could have seen me from anywhere while up on top. There are about four places it’s visible from land, but I don’t know how he could see me at the barn. I can't think of any of those four places you can see the barn area."

"Then there must be a fifth, or he could be watching from an airplane or a satellite."

Tom said, "I guess I could have missed a land-based spot. I don't remember hearing any planes either day, and today it's cloudy like a low blanket. The top of Knobley Mountain's fogged in. I doubt even those secret military satellites can see through today's clouds. It's thick as gumbo."

"Sounds like land-based is the most likely suspect. Mind if I look around out at the barn for where the Benefactor's viewpoint could be?"

"No problem. I have to call Dark Cloud in a couple of minutes. Go ahead and see what you can find, if anything."

"Will do. And I hope things are okay with your father-in-law."

"Me too. I'll soon find out."

Roger got up from the table and walked outside to the barn. Nacho came out and gave him the hungry donkey look. Roger had a half-eaten granola bar in his pocket, and he gave it to Nacho, who strained at the fence. Roger looked around slowly. The cloud cover would help eliminate possibilities. Nothing jumped out at him as he scanned the area around him. Nothing. Wherever it was, it was well hidden. He saw a distant red light flash on top of a mountain that looked like a dinosaur's back. Probably a cell tower. Hard to tell from here. It was worth mentioning to Tom. Could be something. Could be nothing.

He looked around some more, but again, nothing grabbed his attention except a moon-eyed donkey wanting more. "Sorry, Nacho, that's all I have. I suspect you've got a manger full of food in the barn, but would rather mooch off me, right?"

The donkey acted like he'd heard nothing and continued giving Roger the sad face. "Sorry, buddy. I've nothing for you." Roger held his hands out to show they were empty. This seemed to sink into the mule's hard head. He turned and went into the barn.

Roger decided to walk up the trail by the barn that he believed would take him to the top of the hill. The trail was moderately steep, and Roger huffed and puffed as he climbed. He was startled when Tom's three-legged dog ran past him like he was standing still. "Show off," Roger yelled. "Give this flatlander a hard time, will you?"

The dog stopped and turned his head around as if to say, "Slowpoke."

"Okay, okay. I'm coming. Maybe if I had three legs, I could go faster. That and the fact I haven't climbed anything like this in over a decade." Roger shook his head. "Here I am talking to a dog again. My K9 seems to understand. Wonder how many other people talk to dogs?"

Roger stopped often to look around for clues as to where a watcher could be. Clouds covered the top of the mountain knob. He stayed below the cloud cover and looked around. He saw another distant blinking red light beside the closer one. Only from the closer, one could someone see both spots from where Tom had talked to the Benefactor. Roger wondered.

He walked back down to the farmhouse. Again the three-legged dog ran by him like racehorse heading for the finish line. "How does he do that?" Roger said to himself. He saw Tom walking in the kitchen with a phone in his hand. Tom saw him and beckoned him in. "Okay, Dark Cloud. I understand. Can do. I'll work out the details on this end. See you soon. Bye."

Tom set the phone down and looked at Roger. His eyes seemed anxious and maybe even pleading. Roger's curiosity was aroused. "So, what's up?"

"I've got a big favor to ask of you."

“Sure, what do you need?”

“Could you take me to the Pittsburgh Airport tomorrow morning?”

"Yeah, I could. Give me some more details."

“Dark Cloud had a dream. Sarah told him it’s time for her to come home.”

Chapter 20

"Wait, back up the truck and give me some details," Roger said.

"That was Dark Cloud, Sarah's father. He said she appeared to him in a dream and told him she wanted to come home to Dinétah, the land of her people, the Navajos. When she died, I asked him what we should do with her body. I wanted to respect their beliefs and burial traditions. He said the body was now an empty shell and to do what I thought was best. We agreed on cremation. I've had her ashes stored away here at the house until I knew what to do with them. Now I know."

"Okay, this is starting to make sense, but what does it have to do with me and the Pittsburgh Airport?"

"He bought me a ticket. The flight to Albuquerque leaves tomorrow at about noon. I'm taking her remains with me. I'm returning her ashes to the dust of her home. I want to help fulfill her last wish. I need a ride to the airport tomorrow morning. Are you available?"

"Sure. Maybe if I help, Sarah will forgive me for the fiasco I caused when you were in Florida. Sure, I'll help you out."

“Got a place to stay tonight?”

“I was gonna get a motel room in Cumberland or La Vale, but I don’t have a reservation waiting.”

“Tell you what, Roger. You can stay here tonight. We’ll have a good breakfast at nearby Linda’s Restaurant, and then we leave for Pittsburgh."

“Sounds good to me.”

“Only one catch. You get to stay in my daughter’s room. She’s staying with the cousins tonight. I hope you like Dora the Explorer and My Little Pony. She's into that stuff, and the whole room is themed that way."

“Any little pink stuffed unicorns?”

“Probably one or maybe even two.”

Roger said, “Okay, the pink unicorns closed the deal.” He paused. “Would you mind if I cleaned up and went to bed? It’s been a long drive today, and I'd like to turn in early if that would be okay?"

“Do that. I was thinking of doing the same. Jo’s already down for the night, and she’ll probably be up several times tonight with the baby. We can all turn in early and get an early start tomorrow. The bathroom’s over next to Miriah’s room. Lock the back door when you come in after getting your stuff from your vehicle. We can talk on the way to the airport tomorrow.”

“That’s good by me. See you in the morning.”

"Good night." Tom went into the next room, and Roger could hear his footsteps on the stairs. He'd slept in some themed rooms before, mainly with Western and cowboy décor, but this would be a first for Dora and My Little Pony, but the price was right, and he shouldn't look a gift horse or pony in the mouth. Maybe he'd dream of sweet things and sugar plums.

***

The next morning, the men were up at daybreak and sitting at Linda's at 6:01. Their orders came quickly, and they were out of there at 6:30. They crossed the Potomac River into Cumberland, Maryland. Tom pointed to Roger, "Upon that hill where all the steeples are today, General Braddock started his ill-fated journey from Fort Cumberland where he and over 600 of his men died near present-day Pittsburgh. We'll be following much of his route today. How much do you know about these events?"

“Some, not a whole lot, I must admit and certainly much less than you do. You can tell me about it as we go. As I've gotten older, I enjoy history more. It made us who and what we are today. Back when I was in school and college, all I thought about was chasing skirts. History was something to get through, not really learn from.”

“I'll do that. Want some more coffee? I'll buy.”

“Sure, especially if it's on your dime.”

They stopped at the nearby Sheetz store on Greene Street. As they were getting out, a poorly dressed woman approached Tom. “Hello Tom, got time to talk?”

“No Carole, I don't. Can it wait?’

"Yeah, I think so. Could you buy a girl who's down on her luck some breakfast?"

“Sure Carole. Here's a fiver. That enough?”

"Yeah Tom. That's enough. Thanks for all you've done for me."

She hurried into the store. Roger looked at Tom and asked, "Who was that?"

"That's Carole, aka Crazy Carole. She's one of the local street people with mental problems. I try to help her when I can. She's still off her meds, I can tell. She's told me some interesting stories recently. You wouldn't believe them if I told you."

"No kidding? Try me."

"She talks to the Death Angel."

"Really?"

"Really and some of the things she tells me are spot on."

"I know a guy like that in Florida. He seems like he's not quite in sync with the world. He kind of drifts off to another world at times. Say, Tom, just get me a large black coffee, and I'll wait in the car."

"Sure."

A few minutes later, they were on Interstate 68 going west. "Braddock and his men, along with George Washington, cut their way through the wilderness. It was back-breaking work. They traveled a route often parallel to the new road. In places, the highway's covered up Braddock's path. They were lucky to make ten miles a day. At Keysers Ridge, the new road diverges from his trail. US 40 is close to the old trail until Connellsville, Pennsylvania. At that point, it turns north. Some people say this is where the gold was buried. I've heard other stories anywhere from there east to Alexandria where they started. I've heard stories that give credibility to all of these. No one knows where it is today, but lately, it seems to be turning up around Fort Ashby."

“Is that where you think it is?”

“Some of it’s there for sure, maybe all of it, or at least the information to its location. I can feel it in my innards. I think my gut knows where its hidden location is in my head, and it's trying to tell me to get ready for the storm it will set off.”

“You could be right. Hey, look at that!”

Not a hundred feet in front of them, a black bear raced across the highway. "Bear," Tom said. "Getting to be a lot of them. Seems like once a week, there's a report in the paper of one being struck. The bear usually dies."

“First one I’ve ever seen up here in my life. They’re having a great deal of trouble with them around Orlando as the metropolitan area spreads north into bear habitat. Bears frightening residents, eating out of trash cans, and of course, getting hit by vehicles.”

"Up here, deer are a far bigger problem with encounters with cars. The population has exploded, and people are hunting less. If you drive a car in West Virginia or the area, sooner or later, you’re gonna hit a deer or two. You may even see them in your dreams. Hey, swing through Morgantown. I want to see what the old place looks like. Haven’t been there in a while.”

Roger followed Tom’s directions through the town. So much remained the same, but so much had changed. He couldn’t believe where they were building, tearing down the hills and filling in the valleys. They crossed the Star City Bridge and were soon back on Interstate 79 headed towards Pittsburgh. They stopped at the Pennsylvania rest stop where they saw two monuments, one to miners killed in an explosion years ago and one to a mine labor leader who was murdered by his rival. Roger found a brochure on Braddock's Battlefield History Center and showed it to Tom, who said, "Can't say I've ever been there, but I've been told it's a top-notch place."

Roger looked at the brochure. "I think I'll stop on the way back. I should have plenty of time. The viewing tonight's from 6 to 8 PM. Lots of time."

"By all means, do. I like to explore local areas when I travel. I've seen and learned many interesting things. We better get moving. That plane isn't going to wait. The airlines and me have an agreement. They can leave without me if I'm late."

They got back on the highway. Tom found a country radio station, and Willie Nelson was singing about being back on the road again. The boys sang along. They passed Washington, Pennsylvania, and the dangerous turn where Interstates 70 and 79 intersect. Tom told Roger that Perry Como and Bobby Vinton were from Canonsburg as they passed the many small towns. Lots of celebrities were from western Pennsylvania-Jimmy Stewart, Arnold Palmer, Mr. Rogers, Andy Warhol, Joe Namath, Nellie Bly, and others.

Traffic became heavier the nearer they got to Pittsburgh. They exited I 79 onto US 22 West and after a short ten minutes, arrived at the airport terminal. Roger popped the trunk on his car, and Tom took his luggage out. "Hey bud, you have a good trip, and I hope everything works out well for you in the Big Rez," Roger said.

"I do too. I'm not sure what ceremonies Navajos have for death rituals, if any, and all in his family are Christians, so it could be a mix of Indian tradition and Western. I'll find out soon enough. I want to thank you so much for this favor. In some ways, it seems like I've known you forever, and we last talked yesterday instead of over a decade ago."

“We did talk yesterday, but I know what you’re trying to say. I guess that's the way it is between friends." He stuck out his hand, and they shook. "Oh, Tom, I forgot to tell you last evening. I did check on where that Benefactor fellow could be watching you. Me and the dog went all the way up the hill just stoppin’ where the fog engulfed the top. The only place other than from a satellite to see the top of the mountain and also behind the house by the barn was from the top of a ridge to the east where I saw a blinking red light.”

“I know the one you’re talking about. I think it’s a cell tower or maybe a fire tower. I’m not sure which, but it’s been there for some time. It’s probably nothing, but thanks for looking.”

“You’re welcome. Good luck with your task. I’ll stop over at that Braddock’s Battlefield Place.”

“I think it’s correctly called Braddock’s Battlefield History Center. Either way, there should be a map in the brochure.”

“There is. It shouldn’t be too hard to find,” Roger said. “You take care, bud. I’ll give you a call if I find anything that could be useful in solving your puzzle.”

“Thanks. I better go if I don’t want to miss my flight. See you later.” Tom said and walked toward the terminal door.

“Good luck,” Roger yelled.

Tom turned, waved, and disappeared into the building. Roger got back in the car, and the airport became smaller and smaller in his rearview mirror until it disappeared. What would he find at the history center? Lots of information, but would any of it help Tom?

Chapter 21

Roger followed the route through Pittsburgh towards his destination. Traffic slowed on Greentree Hill, barely more than 25 mph with stop and go traffic. At the bottom of the hill, he entered a long tunnel, and to his surprise, traffic speed actually increased. He exited the tunnel and immediately was on a bridge over the Monongahela River. The Golden Triangle, where three rivers met, had been the objective of General Braddock. There Fort Duquesne, the French stronghold, had been. Skyscrapers and a football stadium occupied land where vast and dense forests had once grown.

He took Exit 78 off the interstate and wound his way through the crooked and winding streets of the town of Braddock. The area deteriorated as he drove. The economic revival of Pittsburgh had missed this area. The road grew very rough. He pulled into the parking lot at the Braddock's Battlefield History Center. The building appeared well kept and maintained. Someone was taking great pride in how this place looked.

Roger walked into the building, and a smiling middle-aged man greeted him. "Hello, welcome to Braddock's Battlefield History Center. Have you been here before?"

“No, I can’t say I have.”

“Well, this is the site of the 1755 Battle of the Monongahela during the French and Indian War. The British commander, General Edward Braddock, received his fatal wound here, and over 600 men under him also died in his great defeat. It was Native American’s second greatest victory in American history.”

“Not Custer and Little Big Horn?”

“That battle actually rates as number ten. Most of the Indians' greatest victories were in the eastern half of this country, and few people know this."

Roger said, “You can learn something new every day.”

“Braddock was successful in that he moved a 2000 man army via buffalo paths over mountains and rivers, an incredible task, and almost reached his goal. If not for a perfect storm of events that went against him and his forces, he would have reached his objective and succeeded.”

“Very interesting. Say, this area looks a little depressed today. What happened?”

"This area, battlefield and all, was covered with steel mills. They closed years ago, and it's been an uphill struggle to turn things around. This museum is part of that effort."

“Is there a charge, and could you tell me more?”

"A minimal charge of $5.00. We have a movie you can view of the battle and events leading up to and following it. You can view artifacts found on the battlegrounds. We have a room dedicated to George Washington. His heroic actions in the battle and afterward saved many lives and were one of the main reasons he was asked to become the chief officer of the Revolutionary War Continental Army years later."

"Okay, here's a fiver. Will you be available for questions afterward?"

"I should be. I'm expecting a slow day. Yesterday was crazy. The parking lot was full of tour buses. We'd been expecting some. They called ahead, but the other half merely showed up. I called for help from some volunteers who live local. Even with them, I was stretched thin. It was great for business, but I'm not getting any younger. A slow day would be just fine with me."

"Okay, thanks. I know I'll have questions afterward. Thanks for the information."

"You're welcome."

Roger looked at the exhibits and watched the movie. He learned much, but nothing on Braddock's Gold. In the gift shop, he saw many items for sale related to the battlefield. A book rack held about 40 different books, all connected in some way to the events that had happened here. He purchased a small refrigerator magnet and a T-shirt. Roger saw the man who had greeted him as he left the room. "Do you have some time for a few questions, mister…?"

"My name's Bert Tesser. I'm the curator, tour guide, custodian, and the one who does any other jobs that need doing around here. Last week, I was the plumber who fixed a stopped-up sink P-trap. I do it all."

Roger said, "It's nice to have many talents." He stuck his hand out. "I'm Roger Pyles. I work with the Canaveral Flats and Brevard County Florida Police Departments, Criminal Investigations, and Forensics."

“What brings you to the Pittsburgh area all the way from Florida? Are we under investigation?”

Roger smiled, “No, you’re not under investigation by anyone in the Sunshine State as far as I know. My father-in-law died in the Cumberland, Maryland area. The funeral is tomorrow, and a friend who lives there had an emergency come up. He needed a ride to the Pittsburgh Airport, so I drove him to it. I’m on my way back to Cumberland. He said this would be a good place to stop. I have a few questions. You could be helpful. Have you ever heard of Braddock’s Gold?”

“Yes, the lost gold payroll of the general? Do you want me to tell you where it is so you can dig it up and become rich?”

“Not really.”

Mr. Tesser sighed. “We have people stopping in all the time asking us to tell them the location.”

“Like X marks the spot?”

“Exactly. Have they never thought perhaps if I knew where the gold was, I’d have dug it up myself?”

“That’s funny. Where do you think the gold is?"

“In all honesty, I don’t know. People have argued about what happened to it since the battle. Was it lost? If lost, was it ever found, and by who? What did they do with it? Or is it still lost? If it was buried, where was it hidden?

Just like as with events today, there was a disinformation campaign spun about what happened to it after Braddock's defeat. If it were lost, it would have been in enemy-controlled territory — no point in having the French look and find it. Then shortly afterward, the American Revolution took place, and the Brits would certainly not want their former allies to have it and use British gold against the King and his soldiers. I’ve heard speculation from Alexandria, Virginia, to this very battlefield. I don’t know. All I know for sure is there's a lot of interest in the subject, and it seems to be growing."

“How so?”

"You see articles in newspapers and magazines and even TV on the legend. Why just last week, a gentleman visited and asked some specific and informed questions about the subject. He said he owned a newspaper chain and was interested in publishing a major piece on the legend and mystery of the whereabouts of the lost gold payroll."

“So, do you happen to remember his name?”

Mr. Tesser thought for a moment. “He did give a name. What was it? It started with a G, I think. Hmm, perhaps Golightly or something like that. Sorry, I can’t be more helpful.”

“In your opinion, for what it’s worth, what do you think happened to it?”

"If I were a betting man, which I'm not, I'd say it was lost and may still be out there, but I'm not sure. It seems bits and pieces have turned up since the battle, never a huge cache at any one time, but small amounts years and years apart."

Roger said, “So you think there’s more to be found?”

“I do, but I’m not interested in seeking.”

“Why not?”

“Seems like great riches also attracts great dangers, and I for one, don't think it’s worth the troubles it could bring. I pity the person who would find it.”

Roger nodded, "Yes, I've seen men kill each other for far less."

"The love of money is the root of all kinds of evil."

"Sounds like something my late wife would have said. God rest her soul. Mr. Tesser, thank you so much for your time. It's been a pleasure to talk with you."

"Likewise, Mr. Pyles. I wish you could have been up in this area under better circumstances. May you have a safe trip back home. Sorry to hear about the death in the family."

"He was a good Christian man and is probably at this minute bringing my wife, his daughter, up to speed on all that's happened. And seeing my son, his grandson, again."

"Are you a believer, Mr. Pyles?"

"No, my wife and her family are and were. I'd like to believe they're right. I'm leaning in that direction, but I still have my questions. Maybe, one day faith will overcome my doubt, maybe."

"In that case, Mr. Pyles, I pray you good fortune in your journeys, whether the one back to Florida or your spiritual sojourn. May you arrive safely home. Now, I see a bus pulling into the lot, and I better be ready for the onslaught. I'm sure you understand. Goodbye, Mr. Pyles."

"Goodbye to you, Mr. Tesser. Thanks again for your time." Roger turned and exited the door, but a group of teenagers nearly stampeded him. He got in his car and soon found his way back to the interstate. He hated paying the high tolls on the Pennsylvania Turnpike, but he should have time to think as he drove. *What has Tom gotten himself into? Could anything I've seen or heard while here help Tom? And how's he doing out on the Navajo Reservation*?

Chapter 22

Albuquerque International Airport, New Mexico

“Over here,” someone yelled.

Tom turned toward the sound and saw Dark Cloud waving to him from about 50 feet away. He pulled his luggage behind him as Tom walked over to him. Tom said, “I was wondering how I would find you.”

Dark Cloud smiled, “What did you expect, smoke signals?”

Tom said, “A flaming arrow with a note attached would have worked.”

“I thought about it but didn’t want to set off any fire alarms in the terminal. That and you can’t read Navajo.”

“Good to see you, Dark Cloud.”

The two men embraced. “It is. It’s been a long time Tom.”

“Way too long. How was the drive over from the Rez?”

“Long as usual. My car’s out in the new parking garage. Follow me.”

Tom did as directed. Dark Cloud led him to a dark Pontiac sedan. Tom smiled, "I should have known, a Pontiac."

“Sure, an Indian car for an Indian. What did you expect, a Volkswagen?”

Tom laughed. He had a VW microvan when he had first met Dark Cloud. "Yeah, I should have expected as much." Tom put his bags in the truck, and the men were off through the streets of Albuquerque. “Are you hungry?” Dark Cloud asked.

“Oh, I’m getting there, but I can wait. What did you have in mind?”

“Well, there’s not much till we get to Grants. Does Blake’s sound okay? It’ll take about an hour and a half.”

“I think I can wait that long? How’s Mai?” Tom said.

“Cold feet and warm heart. I told her if she wants to sleep native, at least wear socks. Nothing like cold feet on your back in the middle of the night to get your attention.”

Tom said, “Sleep native? Is that au naturel?”

“Yup, in your birthday suit.”

Tom smiled. “I know. It gets cold in West Virginia, too.”

Dark Cloud laughed. “If you looked at Mai, you’d think she was doing fine. She tries not to let it show. Her diabetes and high blood pressure are barely under control. It’s the curse of the Navajos and many other tribes. It seems like all these modern foods are killing our innards. Our bodies weren’t set up for the white man’s diet. Also, I'm doing pretty good for my age so far. I got lucky and picked parents with better genes. ”

“Glad you’re doing well. It seems like a lot of whites, and other groups can’t handle those items either.”

“True, but it seems the native groups aren’t tolerating it as well. We’ve had less time to adapt to the foods. How are you doing?”

“Other than the PTSD and someone else’s cold feet back home, I’m doing well. Doc gave me a clean bill of health. Thought I was getting’ a cold or the flu, but it seems to be going away. Seems like everyone in my household has it now. Oh, and there’s one more thing; I have a mysterious nemesis. He calls himself the Benefactor. I stumbled on some information that could lead to a large, lost gold payroll. He wants it badly. He's told me he wouldn’t harm my family or me though he did kidnap me and threaten to kill me once. Honestly, I think he would go away and keep his word if I can give him the treasure, but I can't remember. The information went into that black PTSD hole area of my mind and disappeared. How’s that for a summary?”

“More heavy-duty than I expected. Gold seems always to lead to trouble. It’s what got the Navajo kicked off their homeland. When none was found, we were allowed to return. It was a horrible time for the tribe. I don't know if I can be of any help, but let me think about this for some insight, and I'll pray." He paused. "Guess you are wondering about Sarah, and what plans we have for her final sendoff?"

“Yes. Fill me in.”

"It was a big surprise when she came to me in a dream. I woke up with a start afterward. She told me it was time for her to return to the land of the Diné, the Navajo, her home while she lived on this earth.”

“I can understand. There’s no place like home.”

"There was a young man with her who stood in the background. I think it was Brian."

Brian, Tom and Sarah's son, who suffered from mental illness, had taken his own life. Tom said, "I hardly know what to say. I believe he'd be with her. She was the one who could calm his troubled mind. There was a special bond between those two."

"She told me it would be all right. It would all work out. I'm not sure what all she was referring to, but she seems assured and at complete peace when she spoke."

The two men said nothing for a moment. Dark Cloud continued, "I was planning on a simple ceremony with family and friends for scattering her ashes at one of her favorite spots."

"I know the spot. It's up on the Lukachukai Mountain Ridge at the Shiprock overlook."

"That's the one. I want to do it at first light tomorrow. We Navajos have always welcomed the new day."

"Yes, the Bible says, 'After pain in the night, joy comes in the morning.'"

"Yes." The two men were silent for a long while, each lost in his own thoughts. Tom finally broke the silence. "You okay? You mind if I take a little nap? Got up early this morning, and this nasty bug's still telling me it won't go away without a fight."

"You do that. I thought you might say something like that. I'll wake you when we exit the interstate. It's a short hop to Blake's Lotaburger."

"No Blake's back east. I haven't had one of those green chile burgers since I was here last time. Sarah liked them too and tried to find chiles where we were, but finding Hispanic foods in our area was like finding a snowball in a blast furnace. I'm going to enjoy it."

"Okay, it's on me. I think you need to shut up and do put yourself in sleep mode."

"Will do, Kemo Sabe. Over and out."

Tom was out like a light, and Dark Cloud drove on west past the Laguna Reservation, the cut off to Acoma where so many westerns were filmed, and the volcanic flow at El Malpais National Monument. Dark Cloud looked at Tom and pondered. He believed everything happens for a reason. Sometimes it was hard to figure out. He was glad Tom and Sarah had gotten together. Their marriage had been happy, but like most, not without challenges and troubles. Everyone, no matter who they are or what they believe, will have their parade rained on sometimes. It rains on the good and bad evenly. You need to keep looking up to the Great Maker and not your immediate visual circumstance.

Still, it was hard to do that when the crocodiles of life were circling you. He wondered if Joseph ever doubted God still had a plan for his life after being sold into slavery by his brothers. Could he have become depressed when he was falsely accused of a crime, thrown into prison in Egypt, and then forgotten for two long years by a man who promised to help him get out? It's not recorded in Genesis, but young Joseph may have. Peter sure did when he walked on water, but when he looked at the waves and took his eyes off the One, he began to sink. Dark Cloud knew there was a lesson in this.

The miles rolled on as he drove. Tom snored loudly. Yes, he was congested, and it showed. The exit sign ahead read, Grant 1 mile. "Hey, Tom. Siesta's over. Time to rejoin the living."

Tom opened his eyes and stretched. It was a mile off the highway to Blake's in downtown Grants. Tom said, "This community looks like it's seen better days."

“It has. Grants was a boomtown during the uranium rush, but once that petered out and the interstate bypassed the town, it’s been pretty stagnant. There’s a lot of towns like this out in the American West, unfortunately."

The Blake's mascot, a ten-foot-tall man with blue poles for legs, red and white striped jacket, blue hat, and a bowtie, greeted them. He held a Blake’s sign. They pulled in the parking lot and walked in. After a quick bathroom break, they ordered. Tom went for a Lotaburger smothered in green chiles, seasoned fries, and coffee. Dark Cloud wanted two classic burritos with chile sauce, onion rings, and a Coke. After a short wait, a waitress delivered the food to their table. They ate like wolves and quickly finished. Dark Cloud said, "Do you want to drive? It’s been a long day for me already.”

“Sure, I’m feeling pretty good after my nap. I remember the roads to Lukachukai. Any changes I should know about?”

“Are you kidding? Change comes slowly here. ‘Bout like watching grass grow. Oh, Gallup has a new cop running radar near the Navajo’s 9th Street Flea Market. Watch out for him. He’s been writing a whole bunch of tickets.”

“Thanks. Let’s go.”

They got back on the interstate and drove to Gallup. Dark Cloud fell asleep in the first ten minutes. Sure enough, the Gallup cop had someone pulled over, and he was writing a ticket. Tom took several roads before turning on Indian Route 12. The sign had the shape of an arrowhead. He continued on for an hour and turned off at Indian Route 13. Lukachukai was in sight. Tom drove through the town of maybe a thousand. He saw the cemetery where Chris, Dark Cloud's son, laid. Chris had saved Tom's life in Vietnam during the Battle of the Ia Drang Valley. He pulled up to Dark Cloud's home. It still looked the same, maybe a little more ragged, and run down like much of the small town. "Hey, we're here," Tom said.

Dark Cloud stretched and looked at Tom. "I think once we're inside, I'm going to bed. We need to be up about 4 o'clock if we want to be at the overlook and ready by daybreak."

"You show me my bed, and I'll be right behind you."

"Will do."

They got Tom's luggage from the car and walked into the house. Dark Cloud looked for Mai. She was already in bed. He put his finger to his lips and gave a "be quiet" sign to Tom. He would sleep on the couch in the living room. Within fifteen minutes, the men were in bed. Tom laid thinking. *This is where he'd met Sarah. How different his life would have been if he'd reneged on his promise to Chris to tell his father how he'd died in battle. Everything has a reason. Did he believe that? Why had he been drawn into this crazy Braddock's Gold fiasco? When and how would it end?*

Chapter 23

The next morning, Tom and Dark Cloud were up early long before dawn. Tom wore a windbreaker as the crisp low to no humidity air in the high desert held little warmth. He could see lots of stars as he carried Sarah's ashes in its container to the car. Mai was not feeling well and stayed at the house. Dark Cloud drove the Pontiac up Indian Route 13, over Buffalo Pass, and took a short dirt road to an area where cars had begun to park. A steady stream was pulling in.

Tom and Dark Cloud got out of the car. In the dark, it was hard to tell how many people were there, but many lights like fireflies went up the hill. Tom said, "Lots of flashlights."

Dark Cloud said, "What did you expect? Flaming torches?" He laughed. "Besides, we're in a drought, and the tribal council banned open fires. No point in setting all creation on fire. Not a pretty picture."

"Agreed, only you can prevent wildfires."

"Wild Fire? He'll be here."

"Huh?"

"Wild Fire's one of the last Navajos like myself, who was named the old way."

"Oh."

The two men joined the crowd going up the hill. The lights they carried looked like a string of Christmas lights snaking up the mountain. Ahead of them, the lights grew into an ever-growing pool at the overlook. Tom and Dark Cloud continued walking until they reached the overlook. The crowd parted and gave them room. They waited for about another ten minutes as the last of the line caught up with them. The people stood very still in the cold morning air. A woman coughed. A sea of dark faces surrounded them. Tom looked off to the east. A sliver of light was on the distant horizon and touched the top of Shiprock, Tsé Bit'a'í, the rock with wings.

"It's time," Dark Cloud said. "Diyin God Bizaad, Holy God, His Word, long ago, you brought the Diné, the Navajo, to this land, and we first set foot here. Today, we return one of your children to the land. She was away from her first home for a long time, years in our time, but just a moment to One who is eternal."

"Oh One in All and All in One, may we walk in Beauty. With a cool breeze at my face and dew at my feet, we will walk in Beauty. Nothing will hinder me. I will be happy forever. I will walk in Beauty. It will be before me, behind me, above me, and below me. I will walk with Beauty. Your words and face are beautiful. I will walk with Beauty today and forever. In old age, I will walk with Beauty. And when in old age I die, I will walk with Beauty forever. Your words are like honey to my heart, and I will walk in Beauty always. Díí éí bééhózin dooleeł bizhé binajį́ Jesus Christ, Amen."

Many amens murmured through the crowd.

Dark Cloud leaned over to Tom and whispered in his ear, “Trust me on this and do as I say. Get down on one knee and gently pour her ashes over the cliff. Do not throw them.”

Tom was a little surprised at these directions but did as told. After doing this, he stood back up now with an empty container in his hands. Dark Cloud raised his hands and lowered his head. “For we are but made from dust and to dust, we shall all return. You created our frame from the earth, and the dust will return to the earth as it was originally, and the spirit will return to God who gave it.” Dark Cloud lowered his hands. “My daughter’s body has returned to her home in the land of her people, but grieve not. She lives today in beauty with the Great Father in Heaven. Go in peace and may the Lord bless you and keep you until our time has come to travel to where our ancestors are. May peace and Beauty be with you, always.”

More amens came from the crowd. Tom placed the container to the ground behind him. As the group broke up, many people came to Tom and Dark Cloud and wished condolences in English and Navajo. A few had tears in their eyes. One old woman told how Sarah was her favorite student when she taught at the tribal school. Many looked to the rising sun and Shiprock. After about fifteen minutes, everyone had left except Tom and Dark Cloud. They sat down on the cliff edge. Tom spoke, “I think it went well, and I believe she’s at peace.”

Dark Cloud nodded, “I think so, too.”

The men sat in silence for a long time. Finally, Tom stirred. "Sarah's here. I can feel her presence."

“Yes,” Dark Cloud said, “I can feel it, too.”

After a short time, Tom said, “She spoke to me. I saw her face, and she spoke to my mind. I heard her there.”

Dark Cloud asked, “What did she say?”

“She said, ‘It will all work out. You can trust him.’”

“What do you think she meant by ‘You can trust him?’ Who’s the ‘him’ she was talking about, the Lord or this Benefactor guy?”

“I don’t know. I’ve been wondering that too. I know we say we trust the Lord, but do I really do that no matter what trials I'm going through? Or did she mean I could trust the Benefactor, or perhaps both? I don't know. Guess I'll have to wait and see. As she said, ‘It will all work out.’”

“I’m going to have to agree. God’s sovereign and His will shall be done.”

“Yes.”

The two men drifted off back to silence and their thoughts.

A buzzing sound broke their quiet time. It was coming from Tom’s pocket. His cell phone was going off. He pulled it out and answered, “Hello? Roger? I can’t believe I’ve got service. I’m up on top of a mountain. Yeah, maybe that’s why. We just finished up the ceremony. And you? Uh-huh. The funeral there is in a couple of hours. What’s that? You faded on me. Did you say you made it to Braddock’s Battlefield in Pittsburgh? You did. Uh-huh. Find out anything? Uh-huh. Uh-huh. Okay, thanks for following up on that for me. Are you leaving tomorrow? Sorry I won't get to see you. I know — duty calls. Time and tide wait for no man. Thanks. Have a safe trip back to Florida. You, too. Bye.”

“How did you ever get coverage out here?”

“I have no idea. Maybe Sarah has some connections that are out of this world.”

"Could be. What was that all about?"

"That was my friend Roger from Florida. We had a misadventure while I was in his state some years ago and nearly ended up in jail. He had a friend in law enforcement who came to our rescue, but Sarah caught wind of it, went on the warpath, wanted to scalp him, and threatened to turn his favorite organs into a nose warmer and coin purse."

"That sounds like our Sarah."

"I asked him to check into anything he could find about the Braddock's Gold story that happened years ago while he was in the Pittsburgh area. He's also a forensics expert."

"Did he find anything useful?"

"A lot of the usual. No one is sure if it's lost or still exists, but that doesn't stop people of all flavors from looking for it. Oh, he did say the curator at the museum said a newspaperman had been there asking questions, but so what? Isn't that what those guys do? His name, best the curator could remember, was Golightly."

"That mean anything to you?"

"Not really. It sounds vaguely familiar, but I think it's probably another dead end."

"Could be. I think you need to take Sarah's advice, trust. It will all work out."

"I don't think I have much choice. I've got to play out this hand until everyone folds or shows their cards."

Dark Cloud said, "I believe you're right. I'd be ready for some surprises."

"Yup. And I don't think they'll all be pleasant."

Chapter 24

The car ride from the Big Rez to the Albuquerque Airport had been uneventful except for nearly hitting a mule deer that ran in front of them near Gallup. Dark Cloud had little more advice to give him other than stay the course. Sarah had said that it would all work out, and somehow it would. The devil was in the details.

Tom was able to catch some sleep on the flight, and after a strong and large cup of Dunkin' Donut's coffee at the airport, he was wide awake. Tom's son Doug picked him up at Dulles Airport in Virginia. They stopped at a diner on Warp Drive just north of the airport on Virginia Route 28. The area was growing like a well-fertilized weed in a garden, and they concluded the developer who named the roads in the area must have been a Star Trek fan. They saw Federation Way and Enterprise Avenue on the way back to the main road.

This area had lots of American history. Numerous roadside makers reminded travelers of past events. George Washington had been through here many times in his life, from a young man to when he was president. General Braddock and his army had passed this way also.

Many battles of the Civil War happened nearby. Tom remembered stopping at Antietam and walking the battlefield, such carnage, and destruction. He could see how the rolling terrain would conceal vast armies mere yards away from each other. Guns, cannons, and mortars killed thousands in the bloodiest day in American history. He could almost imagine the dead lying on the ground with their grey, clouded eyes open, staring into the sky and hear the blood-curdling cries of the wounded. The nearby house used as a hospital was the eeriest. The pictures of the piles of amputated limbs the surgeons had pitched out open windows were especially moving. After the pain of being shot, the wounded had suffered amputation without anesthesia. If they survived this, disease killed many more. How he was glad, he lived today and not then. At least in Vietnam, they had medics and morphine.

Tom drove after the food break, and Doug quickly fell asleep. The two-lane roads in Virginia buzzed with traffic and an occasional farm tractor going slow and congesting things even more. He crossed the long bridge over the Potomac River, the old C&O Canal, and the busy railroad. Now in Maryland, the roads improved, but not much. Apparently, the high tax state was not spending the money on this area. Maybe they voted the wrong way, and this was how those in control of the state government sought to bring them in line. In totalitarian regimes like North Korea, the message would have been less subtle. Don't send food and aid, the troublesome people starve, and the problem for the elitists is solved. Things here weren't perfect, but how he pitied the people who lived in less fortunate and free societies.

At Frederick, he merged onto Interstate 70 West. Shortly afterward, Doug awoke, stretched, and yawned. “Good nap?” Tom asked.

“Yeah, I needed that,” Doug said. “It’s been a long week with you gone. Wish I could have gone with you. Just glad you were able to go and scatter Mom’s ashes. How was it there on the Big Rez?”

“There’re times I wish I could clone myself and be in more than one place at a time.”

“That sounds like a real recipe for disaster to me. What if your clones had a mind of their own and did their own thing knowing the real you would get the blame?”

“I hadn’t thought of that. I guess it would make a great story for a book or a comic strip.”

“Imagine if Calvin of ‘Calvin and Hobbes’ cloned himself.”

“That’s frightening and even somewhat funny. I don’t think the world’s ready for two or more Calvins.”

“So Dad, how was it?”

“Good flights both going out and coming back. Nothing has changed on the Big Rez. The buildings are looking older and more weather-beaten. A lot of the people are looking similar. Mai isn’t doing well. She’s not looking bad, but the health issues are taking their toll, low to no energy. Rarely does she leave the house. Dark Cloud appeared a little older, but he doesn’t show his age.”

“Must be that Indian blood. Seems the darker the skin, the more protection you have from the sun.”

“True. I’ve known blacks that never seem to age or do it very slowly.” Tom stopped. “Your Mom spoke to me while I was there.”

“Come again? You talked to Mom?”

“After the ceremony on the mountain and as the sun rose for a new day, she spoke to me. Dark Cloud and me sat and mediated. We were silent and completely focused. I saw her face, and she told me it would all work out and that I should trust him. She didn't speak, but I heard her words in my mind."

“Wow! What do you think it meant?”

Tom sighed. “Somehow, it will all work out. I don’t know how, but it will. I don’t know if she was referring to God or the Benefactor fellow when she told me to trust him. I know we can always trust God, and so far, my nemesis has been true to his word.”

“That’s industrial-strength heavy-duty, Dad.”

“It is. This life has its disappointments, often severe. Trucks break down, people do us wrong, relationships fall apart, and those we love pass away.”

“I guess we can hope and put our trust in God. He loves us without conditions, and no matter what obstacles we face, even death. We know we’ll one day be with Him.”

“You can’t lose with Jesus. Even if all goes bad here on Earth and it kills us, we’ll still spend eternity with Him. Even if we lose, we still win when the game’s over. That’s what keeps me going, Doug.”

“Good words, Dad. Keep on truckin’.”

They continued west on the four-lane highway. An accident in the Hagerstown area brought traffic to a crawl for several miles. Blue and red lights flashed as they passed the mishap. It didn’t seem to be too bad, a rear-ender with airbags deployed. Emergency responders were fast at work, and a tow truck was loading one of the participants onto a wrecker.

With the city and the wreck behind them, they drove on. They topped a small hill and were near the Potomac River. On a small knoll to the left, Tom saw something new. He said to his son, “I’ve driven this road for years and can’t say I’ve ever noticed that complex over there.” He pointed with his finger.

“Oh, that place? That’s the Bunker.”

“The Bunker?”

"Yeah, the story has it that the compound's owned by a syndicate or an organized crime family. They made sure the place wasn’t visible from the ground by having lots of evergreen trees around it. A tornado went through here about a year ago and knocked down all the timbers. Didn’t even faze the building.”

Tom said, “And how did you come upon this tidbit of information?”

“From one of the members of the Cumberland Soaring Club. He’s a full-fledged pilot and has flown over the Bunker. It seems like it's an open secret among the flyers. There’s another one similar to it near us. You’d never know it was there unless you knew where to look. It’s concealed that well. It looks like it grew out of the hill and is a part of it. Someone went to great lengths to hide it in plain sight.”

“Where is it?”

“On the top of Patterson Creek Ridge. I’ve flown over it in the gliders the club has. You can see it from our home place. Well, not really. You’d have to know it’s there, and then you’d most likely not see it even then.”

Tom said, “You say it’s up on top of the ridge? Near the fire tower with the blinking red light?”

“Yup, that’s the place, Dad.”

“That’s interesting. Roger was looking around and said the only place he considered the Benefactor could be watching me from, and talking to me at the same time was from somewhere around that tower. You wouldn’t know who owns it, would you?”

“Rumor has it a group called the Flying P Corporation owns it, but I suspect that’s just a front for another shell company that’s a facade for yet another shell company.”

"Like a puzzle wrapped in a riddle wrapped in an enigma."

“That’s a pretty accurate description of it, Pop.”

“Doug, I think I’d like to know more about this.”

"Dad, be careful. Be very careful. You could get into something bigger than yourself."

“Thanks for the advice, Son, but I’m already am up to my neck in just something like that.”

“Dad, enough of this. Tomorrow’s Sunday. What’s on your agenda for tomorrow?”

“Oh, it’s my day to preach at church tomorrow. I’ve been thinking about my talk all the way back from Albuquerque. This one came easy. I think it came straight from the Lord. That's my plan for tomorrow. That and a well-needed nap in the afternoon, but I can’t shake this gut-level feeling that there're some surprises on the horizon.”

“I do, too, Dad. One day at a time.”

Chapter 25

Tom sat on the front porch of his house as the first rays of the sun came across the eastern horizon. He sipped at a large mug of coffee and wondered. A red warning light blinked on the tower on Patterson Creek Ridge several miles away as the crow flies. Was he being watched from there, or was this another promising road that would lead to yet another dead end?

He'd boiled some eggs, got the plates, silverware, and cups out for breakfast. When Joann got up, he'd cook some sausages and get some fresh fruit from the refrigerator. Her cold was better, but the baby was still fussy, and she had been up several times during the night. He would let her get her rest. It would put her in a better mood for the day. Lack of sleep was a sure way to have a grumpy wife.

He heard some footsteps coming down the stairs. Joann appeared. She did not look good. Her hair was in her face, and she squinted in the light. She coughed and cleared her throat, noisily. Tom asked, "How are you, honey?"

"I feel as bad as I look, maybe worse. I feel like I've been hit by a truck. I think it was a hit and run by an illegal in a stolen vehicle who didn't want to get caught if he stopped."

“Ouch, that’s bad, really bad.”

“I feel like a bear that just was woken from hibernation by a hornet sting and then fell off a cliff and planted my face in a tree stump. I think I'm going back to bed. Don't fix anything for me. I'm not hungry. I'm not going to church with you. I don't want to spread any more of this crud around or trade some germs with anyone there."

“Sounds like a good idea, honey. I can handle it on my own. Got a good sermon running through my head, I believe came from the Lord that someone needs to hear.”

She took her hand and brushed her hair away from her face. She nodded and had a pouty look on her face. "Okay. I'm going back to bed. It'll all work out." She turned, and Tom heard her heavy footsteps trudging up the stairs.

He said a little prayer for her and the baby and then fried up some sausages. He quickly ate, cleaned up the dirty dishes, and put the extra sausage he had cooked in a Tupperware bowl Joann had bought from a local distributor in Short Gap. They went in the refrigerator along with the boiled eggs. He got some dog food and walked out of the back door. Three deer were standing nearby. They looked at him for a long moment and then fled up the hill into the woods.

Tripod appeared and snorted as only he could. “Good dog,” Tom said. The dog went right to eating the food Tom put in his dog bowl. His water was fine. Sometimes there was dirt in it from nocturnal visits from raccoons that used the water bowl to wash their food, but it was clear today. Tom walked over to the barn, and Nacho came out. He stuck his head over the fence, expecting a handout. “Sorry Nacho, I’ve got nothing special for you today. Maybe later.”

Tom stroked Nacho's head, ears, and neck, and the donkey seemed to purr even more than usual. "You know Nacho, I wish it was as easy to make a woman purr, but seems like they're a whole bunch more complicated. You usually purr when I do that, but a woman depending on her mood, may want to bite you instead of purring. I'm not sure I'll ever figure them out completely." He stopped. "Nacho, what do you charge for listening to my problems? A psychiatrist would cost me plenty. And remember, we have doctor-patient confidentiality. Not a word of this gets out. It could get me in trouble with certain individuals. I'll see you get a special treat for your time with me today, and last but not least, what do you think I should do with this Benefactor guy?"

Nacho pulled his head up and whinnied through his nose and mouth. Tom said, "That's what I thought you would say. 'It will all work out.'" Tom looked to the east and saw the blinking red light on distant Patterson Creek Ridge. He wondered.

Tom went back into the house and prepared the last of his notes for his sermon. Tom glanced at his planner studying it in preparation for the new week. A glance at the cat clock on the wall told him he'd better be getting ready for church. The clock with eyes that moved from side to side and a pendulum tail had been a gift from Deputy Wagoner to show his thanks for Tom and Miriah's help with animals in need of care and a home. He changed into a dress shirt and some good pants and was out the door. He drove over to Fort Ashby. At the bridge over Patterson Creek, he noticed the creek was running a little higher and murky. There must have been some rain while he was gone.

He turned left at the light, passed the Fort Ashby Volunteer Fire Hall, and less than a thousand feet later pulled into the graveled parking area around the Community Building. Someone was moving inside. Tom recognized him as Tom Pyles. He greeted him at the door. "Hello, Tom."

"Hello, Tom."

“Sounds like an Echo in here, Pastor Tom.”

“Yes, it does, Deacon Tom.” They had worked this identification out to try to cut down on the confusion of who was who at the church. It got even more confusing when the Shanholtz family showed up. Grandpa was Tom Senior. His son was Tom Junior, and his son was Tom the Third. And to even make it more confusing, there were two Marys and a Mary Lou. Somehow they managed.

People trickled in slowly with more arriving just before ten. When the clock hand reached 10 o’clock, Deacon Tom welcomed the people and gave the announcements of upcoming events and told all of the prayer requests. It seemed a lot of the old-timers were not doing well. Mary grabbed her guitar and led the congregation in singing. Joyful music filled the building. During the second song, Pastor Tom noticed three people come in the side door. It was Mr. Godfrey and two brown-skinned people, a man and a woman Tom had never seen before. He greeted them with a smile which they returned.

“Hello, and good morning to you. It’s good to be back in town. Before I get into today’s message, let me tell you a little about what’s been going on in my life. Besides some sickness in the family, Jo and the baby have the flu, and could use your prayers along with many others in the church family who could also use your prayers; I took a quick trip to Arizona to the Big Reservation of the Navajo people. We scattered the ashes of my first wife, Sarah, out there.

“Her father and my father-in-law, a man by the name of Dark Cloud and his wife Mai, could also use your prayers. She has assorted problems, mainly diabetes, and high blood pressure that are wearing her down badly. Please keep her in your prayers.”

A slight groan came from several people. “I call him my father-in-law. Trying to explain how the Navajo see and define the family relationship is different from what you are accustomed to. I asked him once to try to explain it to me, and he smiled and said, ‘It's complicated.' Trust me. It is. I could talk all morning on this and send you home with your head spinning and confused, so I'll spare you that."

Several people grinned, and some looked relieved. “The Bible tells us in the book of Acts which repeats words from the Old Testament book of Joel that old men shall dream dreams and young men shall see visions in the last days. Well, I had a dream. Not sure what it means, if anything, but it was about darkness. There’s darkness everywhere in this world. I could give you numerous examples, but I won’t. You see them too. Darkness is the absence of light. Light is not an absence of darkness. Jesus said He was the Light of the world, and we are to shine that Light wherever we are, not to hide it. I know many here already know that Light. Today, I’m gonna tell you about that Light and give you the opportunity to know Him.

“I’m glad there’s not a Book of Tom about my life like there is about the Kings of ancient Israel and Judah. Fact is, there are three sets of books on them:- Kings, Samuel, and Chronicles and smidgens also in some other books in the Bible. The stories are there, warts and all, the good, the bad, and the ugly. Ahab's given a bad rap, but he was a mighty king who did have his moments. In I Kings 21, we're told of how he humbled himself before God, and this pleased God, but his repentance and obedience didn't last long. Even when the prophet of God, Micaiah, warns Ahab of his upcoming death, he ignores the warning. There's a whole sermon there, but I'll give you the CliffsNotes’ version. Everyone dies. Don’t do it without being right with the Lord.

“I encourage you to do your own reading of the Bible, both the Old and New Testament. You can learn so much. Most people don’t realize that God, through His prophet, told Jeroboam the kingdom David had united would be divided, and he would be the king of the ten northern tribes. God also used a prophet to tell King Rehoboam, Solomon’s son, not to attack Jeroboam and try to recover the land he had lost. And what surprises me, for once in his young life, Rehoboam listened. One last nugget I’m gonna throw out. Did you know we’re not even sure David’s name was really David? David is not a normal form of a Hebrew name. David is very similar to the Hebrew word meaning champion or mighty man. Could it be that he took this pseudonym or nickname as his own just as today we have people who do the same-singers and Hollywood stars, for example? Not sure about that? Good. Search the Scriptures like the Bereans, though you may need some little-known references to check the last one.

“Anyone here realizes I like to digress and chase rabbits?” Tom saw many smiles and nodding of heads. "Yeah, you guys know me. Now let me get down to today’s teaching-‘Do You Not Know?’ You do, don’t you? No? Well, let me tell you the Good News.”

Chapter 26

Tom said, "Open your Bibles to I Corinthians 9:24-27. Here we find Paul teaching using parables as Jesus did. Let me read it, 'Do you not know that in a race all the runners run, but there is only one who receives the prize? Therefore, run that you may have it. All athletes must exercise self-control in all things. They do it to receive a perishable wreath, a laurel for a crown, but we will receive one that never dries up and perishes. We don't run aimlessly about without a firm destination in mind or be like a shadow boxer beating the air. Discipline your body. Keep it under control, lest after preaching this to others, I, myself, should not practice what I preach and in this way, be disqualified, neither finishing the race nor receiving a crown.' You may have had some trouble following that in your Bible. I put several translations together and added a few words to help clarify some points. I hope I did, and you'll not be disturbed that I did.

"Paul's in the Greek town of Corinth when he wrote this. It must have been a sports town as he uses sports illustrations related to running and boxing. If he had been in Pittsburgh, perhaps he'd have used football and baseball and made references to the Steelers and Pirates. Paul compares the Christian life to a race we're in, running to win. The late, great runner Steve Prefontaine always ran with all he had from the very start to the end and, as far as I know, never lost a race when competing in America. He set many records that still stand today. Paul was talking of a runner such as this for an example of one who wins the crown.

“Steve Prefontaine once said, ‘Some people create with words or songs or paintbrushes. I do this when I run.’ One more quote, and I’ll move on. He also said. ‘To give anything less than your best is to sacrifice the gift.’ He was talking about his gift as an athlete, but think and ask yourself, are you giving your best to Jesus for His gift of salvation that cost Him such a price?

“How should we run our race? Earnest, all out, and not half-hearted. Run to win the prize, and above all, make sure you’re in the right race. For example, the Bible asked us, ‘What does it profit a man if he gains the whole world and yet loses his soul?’ Make sure you are in the right race. Only with Jesus, will you be on the right race track.

“And when you run, get rid of all burdens you carry that encumber you, that hinder you, and weigh you down. Gird your loins up so you won’t trip on them and get the best running shoes available.

"Run with endurance. You have to run the whole race to win. Be persistent. Remember the story of the tortoise and the hare. The hare could have lapped the slow tortoise many times, but he took a break and never finished the race. The tortoise was constantly on the move. The hare was not persistent, and he lost out. He never got a reward. Many people get in the Boston Marathon for a free T-shirt printed with, ‘I was in the Boston Marathon,’ but they never crossed the finish line. Don’t be lukewarm. Be like Paul. Fight the good fight. Finish the race. Keep the faith. A crown of righteousness awaits those who endure to the end. The Lord Himself will award it to you and all, not a few or some, but to all who persevere. Don’t slow down till you see His face. Just like the runner, it won’t be easy. All the darkness of this world, all flesh, and Satan himself will be against you, but it will be worth it because of the crown He awards His children.

"So what's holding you back? Do you think you can't do it? Do you think you can't win? Jesus is our Coach, and He ran the race before us. He was our forerunner. Look to Him. Keep Your eyes on Him lest you tire and falter. The prophet Isaiah said we would run and not be weary. We will rise up with wings of eagles.

"In the Olympics not too long ago, two great women runners, Mary Decker and Zola Budd, who were leading the race, had their feet become entangled. The local favorite, Decker, fell and couldn't finish. Budd ran barefoot and suffered a bloody spike wound from Decker's shoes. The crowd began to boo and screamed at Budd. They thought she had made the other runner fall. Budd quit trying to win and finished seventh. This was not the end of their running career. They both ran other races later. What I'm trying to say is this, you may fall and be in pain today, you may be discouraged and want to quit and maybe even have quit, but God is a gracious Coach when disappointment comes. He wants you to rest and heal. Tomorrow is another chance. Get back in the race. He never gives up on you. Go for the gold.

"I've one last illustration. Recently, a movie came out called *Chariots of Fire.* Perhaps you've seen it." Numerous head nodded. "Eric Liddell was a Scotch runner whose running form was best described as 'ugly.' No matter, he ran and won races. In a 400 meter race, he fell. When he got up, he was dead last, but he ran like a madman and won the race by a split second. If you're in the race today, continue on to the finish line. Jesus is there cheering you on. If you're not in the race, you can be today. Invite Him into your heart today and get in the race. Trust Him and make Him your Lord and Coach today. Mary, would you lead us in an invitation song?"

Mary grabbed her guitar and a stool about three feet high. She walked to the front and sat down. "Pastor," she said. "I've something to say. What you said was so right on and spoke to my heart today. I'm a very private person, and I've missed a lot of church recently. I have cancer and have been undergoing chemotherapy." She stopped and took off her wig. She was completely bald. Gasps could be heard in the room. "The doctors told me my hair would fall out. I have a sister in Florida two years younger than me. We look so much alike; we've been mistaken for twins. This wig's made from her hair. To have enough, they had to cut her hair short. She went ahead and shaved it all off to look like me. That's love. No wonder our parents named her Grace.

“So now, you all know. I went to the doctor on Friday, and he gave me the bad news. The chemo isn’t working, and the cancer's spreading. There's nothing more they can do. They've given me six months maximum to live. We all have an appointment with death. My question for you is this, ‘Will Jesus be waiting for you on the other side with a crown?’ You can make sure of that today.”

She began to sing from the book of Habakkuk,

Though the fig tree may not blossom

Nor fruit be on the vine

Though the labor of the olive may fail

Though the fields yield no food

Nor the flocks bring forth their young

Still, I will rejoice in the Lord

Jay Heavner

When my heart breaks over and over

When my loss is too much to bear

Still, I hope for I know you are faithful

And I will rejoice in the Lord

I will rejoice

I will rejoice

In God who is my Savior

Sing my soul

Sing your song of praise

Sing my soul

Sing your song of praise

I will rejoice

I will rejoice

I will rejoice in the Lord

No one stirred. Tom looked around. Many had tears in their eyes. One older woman sobbed. He stood up and stepped next to Mary. He said, “Folks, I hardly know what to say. Mary, thank you for sharing. We will pray for you and help you in any way we can.”

He paused. “We all have an appointment with death. Will Jesus be waiting with your crown of righteousness when you arrive on eternity’s shore? Today is the day of salvation. Get right with your Creator today. Give your heart to Him while you still have breath. Come.”

Five people came forward, and Pastor Tom and Deacon Tom prayed with each who asked for forgiveness of their sins and for Jesus to come into their hearts today. Many people stayed and prayed in the Community Building room. This took about ten minutes. Tom looked around, but he didn’t see Mr. Godfrey and the two people who were with him. They had slipped out while he was busy. How he had wanted to talk to them, and he wondered if the Lord had been working on their hearts today. Right now, only the Lord knew.

Chapter 27

The following Saturday morning

“Señor Boss, wake up. It’s important.”

“Huh? Whaz is it?”

“Sorry to wake you up at 4 AM, but Belle says it is important muchisimo.”

“All right, Jairo. Whazever you saz. Gib me the damn phone.” He handed the Boss the cordless receiver and then left the room. “Hello Belle, why are you calling me? Thiz better be good.” The room spun as he slowly awoke from another night of heavy drinking. He had fallen asleep on the couch in his great room again. “Whaz is it?”

"I'm so sorry to call you at this hour of the night, but we had a problem you need to know about. A patron cut up one of the girls tonight, and we had to take care of him."

The Boss’s head throbbed as he slowly processed the information. “Gib me the details, all of them, and do not spare anything.”

“It was almost closing time, and this new fellow who had been in a few times wanted one of the girls. He picked Nina. You know, the girl from Nicaragua.”

Yes, he knew Nina. She was one of his foundlings and had been there for about a year. Her pimp had been treating her like dirt, beating her, and keeping her strung out on drugs. She was in bad shape as were the rest of the pimp’s girls, all who were illegals. The pimp had been tone-deaf to the suggestions to improve the girl’s treatment or face the consequences. He laughed and shrugged it off. He said he was afraid of nobody, not even God. Shortly afterward, he disappeared never to be seen again, and the girls went to work in the small rooms behind Ned’s Place. They may still be prostitutes, but they had protection, would be treated fairly and could earn their way out of their circumstances if they wanted, if they obeyed the rules, and they stayed off drugs. If not, they went back on the streets on their own.

“So whaz happened?” he asked.

"He wanted to talk before sex and talk he did for a goodly time. He was worried about how she would react, Nina said. When he finally dropped his pants, she saw he was undersized, and she pointed and giggled. That set him off. He pulled out a knife and cut her across her face and breasts. She screamed, and our bouncer, Butch, came running. She got some additional wounds on her arms and hands fighting him off.”

“How iz she?”

“Not so good. We called Doc Brown, and he's busy stitching her up as we speak. He shot her full of painkillers, so she's not feeling it now, but tomorrow will be another story. Her days of working here are over. The patrons aren't going to want a girl with scars all over her."

“How much money duz she have saved?”

“A little over $500.”

“No way for her to continue working?”

“No, no way. What do you suggest we do?”

“You do thiz. She’s from Nicaragua, you say, right?"

“She is.”

“I can make sure she gez back to her homeland, and I want you to douba the money she has when she leaves. You take care of her till she iz well enough to leave.”

Belle said, “A thousand dollars will go a long, long way down there.”

“It will. You know if you do the right thing, I make sure you are taken care of.”

"I do, Boss. You're good to your word. You're one of the few people we can trust not to throw us out or stab us in the back. You're fair. The girls here know it. Follow the rules, and it goes well. Don't do something to disappoint you."

“Correct. I don’t take disappointment well.” He paused. “Where was Big Tony?”

“He was in bed with me. With only one patron, we figured the bouncer could take care of any problems. He did, but we have a room with blood everywhere and a hurt girl.”

“What about the patron?”

“Butch, Tony, and me took care of him.”

The Boss let out a deep breath. He knew what that meant. Someone would be sleeping with the fishes in a deep part of the Potomac around Big Pool if he wasn't already. "Make sure this one stays down. No more floaters."

"No more floaters, Boss. Tony's making sure that never happens again, and I took a souvenir."

"How many now, Belle?"

"Three."

"Anything more, you need to tell me?"

"Just that I'm tired, Boss. I'm tired. I've been doing this for a long time, and I'm tired."

"I am too, Belle. The alcohol's not numbing like it used to."

"Same here, Boss. I've got people cleaning up the mess. We'll have to get the room painted and put new furnishing in. I think the doc is going to keep her sedated and out for hours. If she's stable, I'll have one of the other girls watch her, and I'll try to get some sleep. I'm tired, bone tired."

"I know the feeling. Do what you need to do. Tony will give me his report sometime in the morning. Take care. I will see if I can get back to sleep, but I doubt it. Not going to help these circles under my eyes."

"Okay, Boss. Anything more, I'll let Tony update you on that.

"Very good. Bye."

The phone clicked, and a dial tone sounded in her ear. She placed the handset down in the main phone housing on her desk. How did she ever get here? If someone had told her this was her future back when she was a young and pretty teenager in Fort Lauderdale, she would have laughed in disbelief, but here she was. A young, naïve girl had trusted a man who said he could get her lots of money. He had, more than she could have imagined. It happened so fast; she hardly knew what happened. The price of a virgin had certainly gone down over the years.

She learned she could make money turning tricks, and it made her very popular with the boys in school, but it led her down a descending path. Sex, drugs, parties, and alcohol were her life, and then the cycle began: getting arrested, getting out, and getting arrested again. She kept sinking lower. There seemed no escape until she was rescued, yes rescued, by the Boss's men. She knew she'd be dead if not for him.

She was still a prostitute, but here they treated her well. As she got older, her good looks began to fade, and she became the madam of his place. Some may criticize her for what she had done, but she saw it as a calling. Many girls had arrived more dead than alive, and she had helped save them. It became her mission in life, her reason to live. True, they were all still working girls while here, but some had managed to leave and were now leading regular lives. Some had even married and had children. Maybe someday she'd find a way to depart. Some had not done as well and gone back to the old way. Many of those were dead.

She cared deeply for them all. She looked at the three jars before her on the deck. Each contained a clear liquid, formaldehyde, and a severed penis, one smaller than the other two. Nobody messes with her girls. Nobody.

***

On a hilltop in a building constructed like a fortress, an old man rubbed his eyes and took another drink. It was no surprise to him he was here today. He had seen what the business had done to his father. He had taken the position to avoid war among the various families in the syndicate, and he had done an excellent job at that. Few had dared to step out of line. Swift and harsh correction measures had brought them around and served as a warning to others. They got the point, there had been peace, and the syndicate prospered and grew. But now he was tired, and there was no heir to take over. Eventually, he would be gone, and he had been thinking about his exit. Any way he looked at the situation, he could see no alternative to war among the families. He hoped against hope, it could be avoided, but he saw no other way. He would have to do what he had to do, what he wanted to do. Maybe he could do it his way. Maybe not. The clock was ticking, and he was tired and drained.

At that time, Jairo appeared and asked, "Was it trouble, Señor Boss?"

"Have you ever known a call at this time in the morning to be anything but trouble?"

"No."

"It had being taken care of. A girl got hurt, and I am sending her home to Nicaragua."

"Will she be going to the complex near Jinotepe?"

"I had not thought of that. That is a good idea. I will have to see if it can be arranged." He stopped. "How is Rosa doing?"

"Not so good, Boss. She is very sick. I fear she is dying. She talks in her sleep of going home."

"So here we are. You two have been taking care of my family for years, and now I am taking care of you."

"Boss, we owe you so much. I am sorry I cannot do more around here and take care of her too."

"Do not worry about it, Jairo. I take care of those who are loyal and help me. It is kind of like the movie, *Driving Miss Daisy*. It takes place in the old American South. A black man was hired to see to the needs of an elderly Jewish woman. He did for years, and when his wife became sick, the Jewish woman provided for his family. You remember? It was a heartwarming movie. I liked it very much."

"Yes, I remember when we watch it on the VCR. Rosa cried."

"She did. It was touching. Jairo, I think I will lie down again. I'm so tired. Wake me about nine, and do you think you could have some eggs with bacon ready?"

"Sure thing. Would you want some scrapple also? I found some at Wayne's Grocery."

"I would, and a biscuit if we have any."

"It will be ready for you at nine."

"Excellent, Jairo. I am sacking out now. Check on Rosa and try to get some sleep too. The caretaker must take care of himself."

"I will, Boss. Thank you. I will wake you at nine."

"Good night, Jairo."

"Good night."

Jairo left the room, and the old man sat thinking and wondering. It felt like the calm before the storm. What would the near future bring? There were many ways it could play out, and he was not sure if he could control the outcome. Any decision he needed to make involved life and death. His eyes grew weary. He took another drink of alcohol from his glass, laid his head on the pillow, and was fast asleep and snoring.

Jairo appeared in the doorway. He whispered, "Querido Dios, por favor, ayúdame. Help me. Give me strength. I cannot do it without You. Watch over my boss. He needs Your help and wisdom in the many decisions he must make soon. Please help my wife of so many years. She is one of Your children. Give us peace if You must call her home. Amen."

He left, walked to his room, and lie down next to his sick wife. Again, he prayed. ***Lord, help us all,*** and he was soon fast asleep.

Chapter 28

One week later

The wedding of Frank and Stacy was beautiful. About fifty people attended the ceremony held on the overlook at Cooper's Rock State Forest east of Morgantown, WV. About thirty people went to the reception in the back room at Ruby and Ketchy's Restaurant near Cheat Lake. The establishment had the room prepared, and a lavish spread of food was on a long table by the wall. Everyone seemed to be having a grand old time when Tom felt the call of nature. After a quick pit stop, he exited the bathroom and saw Mr. Godfrey sitting at a table in the central part of the restaurant.

"Why, Mr. Godfrey. What an unexpected pleasure to see you here. What brings you to this neck of the woods?"

He looked surprised and said, "Why, Mr. Kenney, this is unexpected. We have to quit meeting like this. People will become suspicious and think there's more here than what meets the eye." Tom laughed. "Mr. Kenney, I have business interests in the area. You see, I own several newspapers, and now and then, I have to check on them personally. This is a great place for a good home-cooked meal, and I stop in whenever I am in the area. What brings you to this establishment today?"

"A little over an hour ago, I performed a wedding for a friend of mine and his new wife at Cooper's Rock. You may know him, Padre Frank, from the Catholic Church in Fort Ashby."

“Yes, I have heard of him, but I did not know priests were allowed to marry today.”

“They aren’t. It's kind of a long story, and I'll spare you the details. He resigned his position recently and is now working for the police department in Pittsburgh. We're having the reception in the restaurant's private room."

“Could you please sit down, Mr. Kenney? I want to talk to you."

“Okay, I doubt if they will even miss me. They’re enjoying themselves so. I’ve wanted to talk to you too. What’s on your mind?”

“Several things. Could you use some more business?”

“Could I use some more business? Does a pig love slop? Is the Pope Catholic? Does a bear…. well, whatever a bear does. What did you have in mind?”

“My businesses in this area need a good quality bottled water for their employees. I know of no better than yours, but it could be a long way for your servicing. They would need it on a long-term basis and would be getting a large quantity each time. It would probably be every other week. Would something like that interest you?"

“It would. I’d like to hear more. How about I call your office and set up an appointment? Would next week be okay with you?”

“It would. I am not too happy with my supplier now. As their business has grown, the quality of their service and goods has not. I want a natural product, not one from municipal water sources. It is not the same, and you are one of the few in the area who still uses a spring as your source. And, Mr. Kenney, how is the family doing?"

"Like half of the area, recovering from respiratory problems. It tried to bite me too, but never got a good hold. The wife and baby had it pretty bad. Just glad it wasn't the full-blown flu bug that's going around." He paused. "I saw you at my church recently. It was good you could come."

"Yes, I was there with my housekeepers, my majordomos. They are the faithful ones. They have been through a lot in this life and still have their faith intact. I am more of an onlooker, still thinking, still wondering. They encouraged me to get out, and I listened this time."

"Are you living locally now?"

"Yes. I still have a place near Hagerstown, but I have one here where I can lay my hat."

"What did you think of my sermon?"

"Very touching, warm, and moving. I listened closely. I knew you meant every word. I grew up in a big church, and many times it seemed to me the clergy were merely going through the motions of religion. Sometimes they were behaving like the worst of sinners behind closed doors. Your faith is alive and part of you. I admire that in a person."

"Mr. Godfrey, I was just as surprised as everyone there when the guitarist, Mary, took off her wig and told her story. Everyone was shocked, including me. You could have heard a pin drop as she spoke. She's facing her imminent death with strength and her faith. We all are facing death, Mr. Godfrey. We never know if it's years ahead or tomorrow, and we all will pass through death into eternity."

"I know. When I was a young man, I thought getting old would take a long, long time. Now I am old, and it seems like life passed so quickly."

"The Pennsylvania Dutch have many sayings. One is, 'We get old so soon and smart so late.'"

"Mr. Kenney, that is so true. There are tons of truths in those sayings and clichés. Some say they are overused and lack original thought, but I disagree. They make the complex simple and easy to understand."

"I agree. Tell me, Mr. Godfrey. What condition is your soul in today?"

"Now that is not a question I am asked very often. It is complicated, Mr. Kenney, but thank you for your concern. I have some black spots in my past. Do you really think Jesus has enough grace to clean any soiled heart?"

"I do. He said, 'Come to Me all who are burdened and weighed down, and I will make you whole again.' You can be as red as double-dyed scarlet, and He will make you white again, as white as newly fallen snow. What do you say, Mr. Godfrey? Are you ready today to become a new man?"

"You are very convincing, but there is so much to consider. I am not ready yet, but you never know. I could change my mind. Give me some time, and I may come over from my darkness. Please pray for me and continue your good work. Now, you better get back to the reception before they send out a search party. Thank you for your concern."

At that time, a waitress appeared with a big plate of spaghetti, meatballs, and a slice of buttered Italian bread. "Here you go," she said. "If you need anything else, let me know."

"I think someone forgot my coffee," Mr. Godfrey said.

"Darn," she said. "I'll get it. Coming right up. Sorry." She took off like a flash of lightning.

"Enjoy your meal, Mr. Godfrey. I'll keep you in my prayers."

"Thank you. Enjoy your time with your friends, and have a safe trip back to the Cumberland area."

"You, too. I'll give you a call on the business next week. Thanks. See you later.

"Bye."

Tom walked back to the private room. Was it just coincidence that they had met here, or was it a divinely ordained meeting? He liked to believe it was the latter. Everything happens for a reason though seeing it is often like looking through mud. Only later, sometimes much later, are we able to figure it out.

Chapter 29

A big dark-colored SUV drove up the driveway to the old farmhouse where Dan Phares lived. A short elderly man got out. Dan came out of the house and said, “Are you lost, mister, or do you need something?”

The old man looked at Dan. What a sight he was. He never looked you in the eye, and his one hand was withered and pulled up to his chest. A substantial gray beard covered his face, and it appeared to have some of his last meal stuck in it. "Do you still have eggs for sale?"

“I sure do and from free-range chickens. No cages, and they get lots of extra protein from all the bugs and lizards they eat.”

“That would be fine. I’d like two dozen, please.”

“Got ‘em in the basement. Follow me.”

The old man did as instructed. Dan gathered up eggs from a basket and put them in two egg cartons. “Here you go, mister. Anything else?”

“Well, yes. As I was driving up to your farmhouse, I saw a garden full of produce. Would any of that be for sale? I enjoy fresh vegetables. My housekeeper is a Latin wizard with food, and he can make a feast fit for a king."

"Well, yeah. I've got extra. Good crop this year. It'll take a little while. What would you like?"

"I will take a good helping of all of the items you have extra. Can you do that for me, please?"

“I would be more than happy to do that. It’s gonna take a little while. There’s a bunch of them vittles to pick, and I only got one good arm, if you don't mind awaitin'."

“I am in no hurry. I can wait. It is cool in here. Could I remain in the basement? I can sit in that folding chair and be quite comfortable.”

“Well, okay. I got some paperbacks on the shelf, a few by Tony Hillerman, John MacDonald, and Wayne Stinnett. Most of them are by Louis L’Amour. I like those cowboy western, but I think his best was *The Last of the Breed*. It’s a great book about man versus man and man versus nature. It’s my favorite.”

"Thank you, young man, for the information. I will be here waiting for you and them vittles, as you say.”

A crooked smile came to Dan’s face. He grabbed a handful of plastic bags from a bag full of plastic bags and was out the door. Luck was with him today.

This was not the old man's first visit to the old farmhouse. The first time, Dan had accidentally given him something extra in change, a gold coin. He had returned it to a red-faced Dan and pretended not to show his interest in the coin. Since then, the old man had done some inquiring about coins of this kind turning up in the area, and most of them mentioned a strange bearded man with a withered arm. Clues must be hidden in Dan’s farmhouse. Paperbacks lined the shelves, but one book on a top-shelf seemed out of place. He stood on his tiptoes to reach it. He opened it up and immediately knew he had hit gold literally. The pages were old and had a few holes from bookworms, but it was apparent the barely literate author of this thin book was talking about General Braddock's lost gold payroll, and his name was John Phares.

The writer told of how he had helped bury the payroll before the great battle. He was the only survivor of the four men who had placed it in two large cannons near where a small stream entered the Youghiogheny River in Pennsylvania. Over time, he was able to retrieve in his estimation, about 80% of the gold. Some he lost in a river crossing when his packhorse fell. And on his last trip, he could no longer find the location as his landmarks were gone.

He gave 20% of what was recovered to his friend, George Washington, to use as needed during the American Revolution. What remained, he divided four ways. He hid three parts at nearby abandoned frontier forts and. The fourth part, he keeps a nearby field for his and his family's use when they needed some quickly. John had planned on each eldest son in the family tree guarding the secret into the distant future. The first caretaker after him was listed as Jasper Phares.

None was to be used except for dire emergencies. Gold and sudden wealth attracted attention, some unwanted, and possibly dangerous.

At each fort, he found a cracked and abandoned swivel gun which he stuffed full of gold, stopped up the end with a rot-resistant black locust plug, buried it, and then planted a buttonwood tree to mark the location. The old man knew buttonwood was an archaic name for the sycamore tree. Nothing was buried at nearby Fort Ashby by John. It was too close to his farm. He did not want attention drawn to the area and him. The old man began to admire

John Phares for his thoughtful insight. He may not have been a very literate man, but he was no dummy either.

The old man remembered how he had an article planted in the local paper in an attempt to discourage people from looking for the missing treasure. He'd had lead bars painted gold hidden and hidden in various placed in the area where they could be found by the unsuspecting. The paper gleefully reported how the long-missing gold had been discovered and then dutifully said how it had all been a cruel hoax. Interest in the payroll had evaporated and disappeared just as quickly as boomtowns had vanished after the mines had petered out in the old West.

Today, he'd found his answer as to where the gold treasure was. The missing gold was in three locations-Fort Cocke, Fort Nichols, and Fort Seller. He had done his research, and he knew the location of Fort Cocke had been lost to time. Fort Nichols was in nearby Maryland at the site of the old Celanese Fibers plant. The state of Maryland had the factory razed a decade ago, and a prison was located there today. He felt he knew a way, if needed, to get in to look around. And lastly, Fort Seller's location was near the town of Patterson Creek in West Virginia. Pieces of the puzzle were fitting together. He now knew why someone lured Tom Kenney to the farm where his syndicate's marijuana grow-house was. He knew where the treasure was. Tom's kidnappers were forcing Tom not only to be digging his own grave but also to unearth the payroll. It made sense.

He heard a rustle outside. Dan was coming. The old man closed the book and slipped it back in its slot on the top shelf. A moment later, Dan appeared. "Man, it's hot out there, but I got your stuff. Got some maters, carrots, corn, cukes, and some beans. Ten bucks should take care of it all."

The old man took the bounty from Dan's one working arm and laid it on an ancient table. "Here you go, young man." He reached into his wallet and produced a ten-dollar bill which he handed to Dan. “I thank you very much. You have provided me with more than I expected." He paused. "I was here once before purchasing eggs, and you accidentally showed me a gold coin. Do you have any more, and would you be interested in selling them at a fair price?"

Dan grimaced. “I thought you looked familiar. That was some time ago.”

“Yes, it was.”

“If I did, what would you offer for one? They’re valuable, you know.”

“I know. Would fifteen hundred dollars be agreeable?”

Dan's eyes widened. "Yeah, that's a lot more than the coin dealer in Cumberland gives me."

“I am offering you a fair deal, not a rip-off. What do you say?”

Dan thought for a moment. “Sure, and I’ll throw the veggies in for free.”

“Done,” the old man said. He peeled fifteen one hundred dollar bills off a wad he pulled from his front pocket. “This is my lucky day.”

Dan pulled a gold coin from his pocket. “That’s my last one, my lucky one. I don't wanna sell, but I really could use the money. So, it’s all yours. Thank you.”

“You are quite welcome. I think I will be on my way. I have much to do. Have a good day.”

“You sure made my day. Thanks again.”

The old man walked out of the basement and got into his SUV. He turned around, waved to Dan, and then drove down the farm lane to Dans Run Road. He made a left and soon disappeared. Dan put his hand in his pocket and felt the money. He mumbled to himself. “I sure needed the money. Wish I had more to sell him, but you can’t have everything. Hope it brings him as much luck as it has me. I wonder who he was?”

Chapter 30

“Well Tony, what went wrong?”

"You know Boss, I've been asking myself the same question, and I keep coming back to this; we followed procedure and did everything by the book."

“Are you certain?”

“I am. I’ve looked at this from every possible angle. The only thing I think would have changed the outcome was to have been in the room with Nina and the john, and I'm not even sure with doing that; we could’ve prevented her from getting cut.”

The Boss said nothing for a moment. Big Tony had a nervous expression on his face. The Boss broke the silence. “I agree.”

Tony breathed a sigh of relief.

The Boss said, “Always stick with the plan and if it falls apart, have a fall back plan and improvise if you must. You did everything correct.”

The two men said nothing as the Boss continued to drive westward on I 68. When they were on the crosstown bridge in Cumberland, Tony asked, “Where are we going?”

"Western Maryland Correctional Institute, your old home."

"Ah, yes, the good old days. That was a cake gig if I ever had one."

"Yes, you did very well there. We did lots of favors for the warden, made him look good, and we were able to recruit a whole bunch of soldiers for my organization. You have performed well for me. I reward those who do good work. Never disappoint me."

"I know better than that. What business do we have at the prison?"

"Years ago on the land where the prison is now, stood the old Celanese Fibers Company Plant. Many, many years before that, a stockade fort stood somewhere on the site. Its name was Fort Nichols, and I have reason to believe part of General Braddock's lost gold payroll is buried somewhere at that location."

"Braddock's Gold. You think you've finally found it?"

"I do. I believe it is there."

"That payroll has sure caused a whole bunch of trouble and a lot of deaths."

"Yes, you would know."

They took exit 42 onto US 220 south. Two miles later, they turned left into the visitor's parking lot at the prison. They walked to the guard station. A guard said they were expected and took them to the warden's office. The guard shut the door and left. Warden Clinton spoke, "Well, this is an unexpected pleasure to see the both of you here, especially you, sir. I've heard so much about you." The Boss smiled but said nothing. The warden stuttered as he started, "What brings you here today?"

The Boss said, “I need to call in a favor.”

“Sure,” the warden said. “What do you need?”

“I need access to the entire prison. I need to look around.”

The warden looked puzzled. “That’s all? You need to look around. I was expecting something big.”

"I am looking for something, and if I should find it, I want you to see I get it, and no questions asked. There is to be no record of us being at this location today. Is that clear?"

“Sure. You’ll need an escort so you won’t be stopped.”

“Make sure it is one who can and will keep his mouth shut, one who knows this prison like the back of his hand.”

“Mr. Smith is just the man you need. He used to work at the old factory that was here before. He got a job doing the demo work and then in the construction of the new place. When that job ended, he got on as a maintenance man.” The warden pressed a button on his phone and said, “Gladys, get Mr. Smith up here ASAP. I have a special job for him.”

“I can have him there in less than a minute. He’s out in the hallway changing light bulbs,” came the female voice from the speaker.

"Perfect, Gladys. Tell him to come in when he gets to my office, no need to knock today.”

“Roger, I’ll tell him.”

“Would you like to tell me what it is you’re looking for? I may be able to save you some time.”

Coldly, the Boss replied. “That won’t be necessary.”

At that time, a man dressed in coveralls of about sixty years of age entered the room. "You asked to see me, Warden?"

"Yes, these two men need an escort. They're to be given access to all areas as they required, and there's to be no record of their presence at this location today. Do I make myself clear, Mr. Smith?"

"Yes, sir. Like Sergeant Schultz in Hogan's Heroes, I see nothing."

"Good. Provide for their needs. Do what they ask. Take them for a meal at the staff's cafeteria if they would like."

"I will, sir." Mr. Smith looked at the two guests. "Are you gentlemen ready to go?"

"We are," the Boss said. "I am anxious to be done with this matter. Let us go."

The three men exited the room. When the door shut, the warden mumbled under his breath, "I hope this works out." He shook his head and sighed deeply. "Could be a world of hurt if it doesn't."

The three men walked down the hallway and stopped at a restroom. The Boss said, "We better stop here and take care of our human needs."

"Okay," Mr. Smith said. "I just drained my weasel before I got the warden's call. I'll be out here waiting for you."

The two men went in and stopped at urinals that were side by side. Big Tony spoke, "Boss, how will we know when we see Braddock's Gold? What's it going to look like? Will it be in a chest or what?"

“It was buried in a swivel gun.”

“What’s a swivel gun?”

"A small cannon used as an antipersonnel weapon. Quite deadly at close range."

An idea came to Big Tony, and he asked, "If it's been buried for 250 odd years, what would it look like today?”

“Rather ordinary, like a rusty old piece of pipe approximately three to four feet long. And very heavy.”

“Boss, when you had me here before, and we were building the new structures, we found something like that. We couldn't believe how heavy it was."

"The gun itself weighs much and full of gold; it would take several men to move it, let alone carry it." The Boss looked at Big Tony. "You think you have seen it?"

“I know I have, and I know where we reburied it, down by the river under the extra dirt we dumped.”

"Interesting. We will do this. We will walk a winding route through the prison and work our way down to the river. Do a lot of inspections and observations on the way. We do not want Smith or anyone else to know what we are looking for.”

“Sounds like a plan, Boss.”

The two men exited the restroom and found Mr. Smith waiting. “Let us proceed,” the Boss commanded.

The two men took their time walking and looking at many things as they meandered through the vast prison. As they neared the swift Potomac River, cliffs of Knobley Mountain towered above them on the West Virginia side. A temporary fence and a guard armed with a sawed-off shotgun stopped them. "This is as far as you can go," he said.

"Charlie," Mr. Smith said. "These men are guests of the warden. I was escorting them and told them they're to be allowed a complete and free run of any place at the prison. That directive came straight from the warden's mouth. And he said to forget they were ever here."

Charlie's eyes widened slightly. "Alright. The warden's word is law at this facility. You may pass. Be careful. The reason this little fence and me are here is the floods washed away the perimeter fence. It's dangerous past this point. The river took out about fifty feet of land and the bank's undercut. Don't get too close. The flash flood down Warriors Run some time before washed out a bunch more. Be careful. The water's running high, and you'd likely be swept away and drowned. That would be hard for the warden to explain, so use caution. I like my job and will be retiring soon. Don't need no black marks like getting fired for not stopping you. I'd make a convenient scapegoat for him if something went wrong. Please be careful. Okay, guys?"

The Boss said, "Thank you for your concern for our safety, Charlie. We will not be long, and we will be careful." He turned to Mr. Smith. "Mr. Smith, you can remain here. There's no point in you coming with us. You stay here, and we will be back soon."

Mr. Smith said, "Will do. I need to talk to Charlie about the football game, and Steelers beat Baltimore. I'm a Pittsburgh fan, and he roots for the Maryland team, and I want to rub it in."

"Sure you do," Charlie said and laughed. "Just remember only one of us has a shotgun, and it ain't you."

The other three men laughed also. The Boss said, "You guys play nice." He looked at Big Tony. "Let's go."

Big Tony took the lead and walked down near the edge. He looked around up and down the river and frowned. "Not good."

"What is wrong?"

"We dumped it down here alright, but where we dumped it ain't there. It's gone."

"What do you mean?"

"The land used to go out at least another fifty feet. It's where we placed the extra dirt we got from doing construction here at the prison. We filled a ravine that was a good twenty feet deep. It's all missing. And that's where we buried the old factory machinery we dug up, and the piece of pipe I now know was a swivel gun. Everything's gone."

"And it is now somewhere between here and Cumberland and probably buried under many feet of soil and rock. We will never find, and no one knows where Fort Cocke is today. That leaves only one cache still out there."

"Sorry to give you the bad news, Boss. Think anyone will locate that last cache?"

"Maybe. It is possible."

"What do you think that part would be worth today?"

"About a quarter of a million dollars. I think people are not going to stop looking for it."

"Me too Boss. Me too."

Chapter 31

Tom sat in his truck in the parking lot at the Berean Baptist Church in Fort Ashby, West Virginia. It was his second recent visit. He thought about the conversation he'd just had with the pastor about the gold found on the property and nearby. Dan Phares' name kept coming up.

The gold found at the church now sat securely in a safe deposit box at a local bank. They were not sure as to who owned it or what its ultimate fate would be. The land the gold turned up on was purchased from the Phares family years ago.

Tom looked up at the old farmhouse Dan called home. It looked even more weathered than before if that was possible. The only thing that looked well taken care of was the nearby garden. Dan seemed to have a green thumb. He could see chickens running around the property. Some pecked at the ground. One raised her head and swallowed something, probably a lizard or a large bug of some kind, and two other hens fussed at each other. They didn't see eye to eye on something.

Tom needed to talk to Dan. He seemed to be the hidden key to this mystery. And the Kenney household needed some eggs. He started the old truck up, pulled onto Dans Run Road, and traveled about 500 feet. He took a left on the farm lane that leads up the hill to Dan's abode. Tom got out of the truck and walked up the rickety steps to the sagging porch. He rapped on the door. It looked like it hadn't seen new paint in thirty years or more.

He heard some sounds inside. The door opened, and there Dan stood with a gun in his good hand.

“Whoo, Dan. No need for that. It’s me, Tom.”

"Sorry," Dan said. "You caught me in the middle of a nap. I was havin' a bad dream, and I thought you were those pukes who came around last week. Troublemakers they were. I told them never to come around if they knew what was good for them, and I meant it. What do you want?”

“Couple dozen eggs and to talk to you about something important. How’s business been?”

"Been picking up. I should be okay for money for a while. Do you want brown eggs or white eggs? Same price for both?"

“How about one of each?”

"I can do that. You need any veggies? I got a good crop this year, and I got surplus for sale, maters, cukes, corn, and some beans, too, that kinda stuff.”

“I think the eggs will be fine.”

“Okay, got ‘em in the cellar. Eggs keep better down there."

The two men walked down to the entrance to the cellar and went in. On an old table sat cartons of eggs marked brown or white. "Take one of each," Dan said. "That'll be four bucks, please."

Tom gave Dan a five, and he reached into this pocket with his functional hand. He pulled out a wad of bills, and as he did, many coins fell to the floor. He handed Tom a one and said, "Guess I need to make a trip to the bank."

Tom helped Dan pick up the coins. “I don’t see your lucky coin, Dan.”

He replied sheepishly, “I sold it. That’s why I need to get to the bank.”

“You sold it? To who?”

"A fellow who had been here before. I guess some time ago when he was here buyin' eggs, and I accidentally gave him a gold coin as change, so he already knew I had it, and he offered me lots of money for it. It was my last one. I didn't want to sell it, but I really needed the money, so I did.”

“What did he look like?”

"Oh, a pretty ordinary older fellow, kinda short, and he was driving a dark and big SUV with tinted glass. He was the kind of guy you would have passed on the street and never thought twice about. What’s the big deal?”

“What’s the big deal? Did you know the church down the hill just found a box full of those coins?”

“No, I ain’t been down there since I put one of those coins in the offering plate. I was too embarrassed to go back. Why you givin’ me a hard time?”

"Dan, you could be in big danger. People are looking for Braddock's treasure, and they're not all nice people. Some would kill for it. I know."

“Yeah, you should know about that after what you told me when you were here in this very room last time. Don’t you remember?”

“What are you talking about? What don’t I remember?”

“You don’t remember, do you?”

“No, what don’t I remember?’

"In this very room, you told me never to tell anyone about the old book on the shelf. You remember now, the old one that tells how my ancestor recorded how he retrieved Braddock’s lost gold payroll after the battle up in Pennsylvania and brought it here. He then buried it at Indian forts nearby and planted a sycamore tree on the spot to mark it. Now you remember?”

Tom's jaw dropped as Dan's question sank it. The PTSD fog that had clouded his memories slowly lifted. Yes, he remembered. He saw it, and he saw it all.

He remembered getting kidnapped and nearly dying twice at the old farmhouse at the north end of Patterson Creek Ridge. And he recalled his conversation with Dan on never telling anyone about the book or the treasure. And he remembered his promise to tell his nemesis, the man who called himself the Benefactor, that if he regained his memory, he would notify him of what he knew and all he knew about the missing treasure. Tom knew he would, but this presented another problem. With this information, the Benefactor would no longer need him. He was expendable. Would the Benefactor be true to his word and see that no harm came to him and his family or not? Just like in his dream, things were coming to a head.

"Yes, I remember." He let out a deep breath. "And now I must do something I promised I'd do and trust everything works out. I have much to consider."

"Glad we have that cleared up. Now, could I ask you for a favor? Would you give me a ride to the bank in town? I need to drop off all this money."

Tom was slow in answering. "Tom, you okay?" Dan asked.

"Oh, sorry. I felt like I was in a trance. All these thoughts were running through my head at a million miles a minute. Sure I'll give you a lift. I was going that way anyway."

Tom grabbed his eggs, and the two men went to the bank a mile away. Tom waited outside while Dan did his business inside. Dan said he was okay with walking home, but Tom talked him into letting him drive him back. Dan said he wanted to stop at the Berean Church because he needed to speak to the pastor on a personal matter, so Tom dropped him off at the front door.

As Tom drove back toward his home, his mind wasn't entirely on driving. It raced as he thought about all the possibilities that had opened up. How was this all going to end? A shudder went through him as he mused on what might happen. He was going to have to play this one out and hope and pray for the best come what may.

Chapter 32

Early the next morning at the Fortress

The old man was up early the next morning before daybreak. He'd slept in his bed last night and not fallen asleep on his couch in the great room of the Fortress. He'd drunk some the night before, but not his usual amount that put him in a stupor.

He dressed quickly and crept into the oversized kitchen. The aroma of coffee drifted to his nose. Jairo must have prepared the new programmable Mr. Coffee, coffee maker. The old man knew he hadn't. Just the same, he would not let it go to waste. He grabbed a sweet roll a local shop, Caporale's Bakery, had made and tasted it. Delicious. The first one went down fast between sips of black coffee, and he grabbed a second one and two pepperoni rolls. The old man put them in a large plastic bag. He poured the rest of the coffee in a large thermos.

A noise surprised him, and he turned and saw Jairo standing in the hallway doorway. "Señor Boss, what are you doing up? It's my job to prepare your breakfast. Go back to bed and get your sleep. I take care of this."

"No, Jairo. I'm pulling rank on you as the boss. You go back to bed. I'm going outside for a while. You go back to sleep. Take care of your sick wife. How was her night?"

“She do better. She sleeps more each night and is feeling close to normal. Perhaps the cancer treatment is working.”

“I hope so.”

“Boss, I must fix you breakfast.”

“No ands, ifs, or buts. Go back to bed.” Jairo looked disappointed and somewhat surprised. “Tell you what, Jairo. I will be back in around nine. Have breakfast about that time. Is that good for you?”

“It is. I have your usual prepared and more coffee, too. I see you found the sweet rolls I purchased. How are they?”

“Delicious. My only regret is you did not find them sooner.”

Jairo smiled. “Good. Where you be if someone calls? What I do?”

"I will be in the fire tower most of the time. Forward any calls that are life and death there — nothing to my cell phone. I want some quiet time, so hold anything else. I will take care of it later.”

“Sí, Boss. I do that. Enjoy your walk and peace.”

“I will. Now, you go back to bed as ordered.”

“Okay, Boss.”

Jairo left the room, and the old man grabbed his thermos and the plastic bag containing the goodies. He walked down a set of steps to a long hallway. On either side were many doors. One led to the washroom. In another room, large electric boxes hummed, and in a third, Tom Kenney had been held and threatened with death if he didn’t divulge what he knew about the lost Braddock’s Gold payroll. He had failed to do so because he couldn't remember. He claimed his

PTSD prevented him from doing so, and the old man had believed he spoke true.

Nevertheless, he knew something somewhere at some time would trigger his memory, and Tom would tell him what he knew. He felt it. It was all coming to a head and soon.

The old man walked down the long hallway, took a right to the heavy metal door, and opened it. A short tunnel led to the outside. He walked to the entrance and carefully looked out. Two deer browsed a short distance away. The old man remembered how, shortly after his wife had died, in a fit of rage, he had killed many deer nibbling on her rose bushes. The first three went down with one shot from his large-caliber rifle, and he killed two more before the others bounded away. They had finished off the last of the venison not too long ago.

He walked out into the open, and the deer scattered. The fire tower was a short walk to where it sat on the very highest point of Patterson Creek Ridge. Within its four steel legs, were a series of long stairs, six in total, that lead to the little room on top. By the time he made it to the top, he was out of breath and was definitely feeling his age. He opened the trap door and went inside. From about four feet up, the walls were glass on all four sides.

The tower appeared to be an ordinary fire tower at first, but cleverly concealed antennas and satellite dishes revealed its real purpose. From here, the old man could control his vast syndicate and issue orders and directions necessary to keep things running smoothly if he needed, though he much preferred the climate-controlled information room in the Fortress. From the fire tower, he could see in real-time any place in the world.

He'd viewed the shootout at marijuana grow-house nearby some years before. He still wasn't sure about all that went on that day. Pieces in this picture puzzle were still missing, but he was sure of several things. It was too close for comfort to his headquarters. Two men died needlessly, and he had lost a valuable commodity. And one last thing, Tom Kenney had been present when this had all gone down and was a key player if not the key player in finding Braddock's Gold.

A blinking red light warned low flying airplanes; though on maps, this area was officially a No-Fly Zone. It was interesting what you could do if you knew the right people and they were beholden to you.

The Fortress had been his creation and baby. He spared no expense. It was similar to the place known as the Bunker, an hour's drive away in Maryland. It was a lot closer by the way the crow flies, but this place was chosen for its seclusion and privacy. He had used as many earth-friendly materials as possible to make it blend in with the surrounding area. There were four ways in, but only one visible and the Fortress could be easily defended if need be. Jairo had recruited a group of illegal aliens who worked hard and were paid well to work and keep their mouths shut about their work. Three different tunnels led three different ways for escape routes.

The east route led to a distant shed where an escape four-wheel-drive vehicle waited for any emergencies. The south route had motorcycles stored at an outdoor lean-to ready and waiting for use, and the west route led to the old quarry near the gentle stream of Patterson Creek. From a book by a local historian, he had learned in 1908 an Italian immigrant had purchased the land and started a limestone quarry. There was only one problem; there was no limestone. The would-be quarryman had never tested the rock. It was only sandstone that looked like limestone. In a short time, the endeavor went belly up, leaving the massive concrete structures built to process the stone as memorials to poor planning and broken dreams. The old labyrinth remaining made a great place to end another escape tunnel.

The west tunnel split in two. The second exit on this tunnel was high on the steep side of the ridge. A long cable ran steeply down to a two-story barn located in the wide bottomland of Patterson Creek. It had a big door on the top floor. A high powered truck waited inside to provide for a quick escape. The same company that had built the emergency escape system for the launch towers used in manned flights at Kennedy Space Center had made these. Two people could use it at once if need be. This was one he hoped never to use. In tests, the doors at the bottom had failed to open, and the escape pod had crashed through the door, and in another trial, the brake had failed, and the pod had gone through the other side of the barn. One brave man, an ex-Navy Seal, had successfully ridden it down, but was so terrified by the ride, he'd wet his pants. Never again he vowed, never again. The old man knew he would never use this option unless it was the only one left.

The Fortress had been his home for many years. A massive fortified gate guarded the gravel road leading up to it. It was here his daughter fought and eventually lost her battle with lupus. She never left the Fortress while alive. Sunlight worsened her condition. The disease weakened her kidneys and finally took her life. After her death, her mother suffered chronic depression and never recovered. She pined her life away and died of a broken heart. The very place he had built to be a fortress from the cares of the world had become a place of suffering and pain for him. Never was it attacked from without but always from within. Now he was alone and the head of a crime and intelligence-gathering operation that would make James Bond green with envy. He had money and power like Solomon, but what had it gotten him? Certainly not happiness. There had to be more. There had to be. He knew it.

The Sun was now above the eastern horizon. It was going to be a beautiful day. A slight breeze blew from the west, and he knew from past observation, it would pick up in the afternoon. He programmed the view screen onto the Kenney homestead a few miles away. He saw a jackass near the barn eating grass and a three-legged dog hopping around. Someone had pulled into the parking area by the barn. The workday at Knobley Mountain Bottled Water Company had begun. He wondered if this would be the day Tom would remember about the treasure.

He poured some coffee from the thermos and sipped it between bits of sweet roll. He thought about what Tom Kenney had told him and laughed to himself as he had seen Tom's face redden when he realized what he had said about his ass and the apple core. Indeed, he had been embarrassed. And Tom’s reference to the Phoenix and darkness-how could he know?

And yes, he wanted the gold, but not nearly as much as he had before. With his grandfather, it had been an obsession, and because of that, his own father had tried to dissuade him and anyone else from pursuing, but it had done just the opposite. As they say, forbidden fruit is always sweeter.

He thought about what Tom had said about forgiveness. It was open to all. Jesus turns no one away, not even a man like him. The burdens he carried were the size of Mt. Everest. Could he ever be free?

He looked over his vast holdings and thought of all his wealth hidden in so many places offshore and the power he possessed. People would live or die if he so wanted. Powerful men in government and foreign lands could be brought down with a carefully planted leak, story, or word from him. All this, and he still felt empty. ‘Vanity, vanity, all is vanity,’ Solomon had said. Solomon started well but didn't end well. The old man didn't want to be like him, but if he continued down this path, he would. Something had to change, and he knew what he had to do. It could cost him his life and everything he had, but he knew nothing good comes without a high price. It cost Jesus everything.

The old man looked at his watch, 08:45. Jairo would have his breakfast ready by now or very shortly. He shut down the computer equipment he had been using, opened the trapdoor, and trudged down the steps of the tower. He walked to the Fortress and opened the heavy outer door. The long hallway was gloomy, but he did not notice. At the stairs, he smelled bacon. He bound up the stairs and entered the kitchen. "Hello, Jairo. Prompt as usual. How's Rosa?"

"Still sleeping, but she is feeling better. I have your breakfast ready for you."

"I can see that. Put a lid on it. I have something important I need to speak with you about."

A look of uncertainty came to Jairo's face. "Okay, Boss. What do you need to tell me?"

"Not tell you. Ask you. Do you honestly think the salvation Mr. Kenney talked about is available to a man such as I?"

"Any man, any woman can come to Him. Come by faith. He refuses no one."

"I think so, too, but it will cost me everything. I cannot go on like this. My life must have a new direction."

"I know Boss, but you are growing old, and you cannot take any of it with you anyway."

"I know. Vanity, vanity, it's all vanity. I want a new heart today."

"Then pray to God. Ask Him to clean your heart and make you anew."

The two men prayed together. Tears flowed down their faces. The old man said, "I've done it, and I feel like a new man. Something has happened. The millstone I carried on my shoulders is gone. Thanks be to Him."

Jairo smiled, "Boss, you make me feel like I did when I prayed for forgiveness long ago. Freedom, Boss, it's real freedom."

"Yes, freedom. I cannot continue down the old path, Jairo. I must change, and it will affect you, too."

"I knew that Boss, but it is worth it. What do you have in mind?"

Over the next ten minutes, the old man told Jairo of his plans. Jairo said nothing but nodded in agreement several times. Concluding, the old man asked, "What do you think? Will it work?"

Jairo stroked his chin. "You know Boss; it just might work."

"Then start making arrangements right after we eat. It must be done quietly. We must do nothing suspicious or out of the ordinary. Leave nothing to chance. I will do my part. I trust you can do your part."

"Sí, our very lives depend on it."

"I know."

Chapter 33

That evening

Tom sat at the picnic table by his bottled water business warehouse, and he was nervous. He knew how the proverbial cat on a hot tin roof felt. He wanted to get off badly but was afraid of where he'd land once he jumped. Out of the frying pan and into the fire, his late father would have said. Was he signing his death warrant by giving the Benefactor the information he now knew, or was this going to end his nightmare? Either way, it was moving forward. He couldn't turn back. It was coming to a climax and an end.

He dialed the number the Benefactor told him to use, 000-000-000, but he stopped and did not dial the last 0. Tom pressed the end button on his cell phone and laid it down. He let out a deep breath, picked up the phone, and redialed it, 000-000-0000. There, he'd done it. He listened as the phone rang in his ear: one, two, three rings. Maybe he wouldn't pick up. Four, five. On the fifth ring, someone picked up. "It is you, Tom." came the altered voice.

"Yes, it is. You said to call if I had information on Braddock's Gold. I remembered. In an instant, it all came to me like a shot out of the blue."

"Well, well, that is pleasant to know. I have waited so long for this moment. What do you have for me?"

“My sources tell me around half of the gold has either been lost or used since it disappeared 250 years ago. The lost part is gone unless someone can figure out where it was lost, and that trail has been cold since shortly after Braddock's death. The used up part is just that, used, spent, and gone. The rest lies buried at French & Indian War forts around the area, and I think those caches are still at those sites to awaiting discovery."

"Now that is excellent news, Mr. Kenney. Are you sure about half has disappeared and gone forever?"

“I’d give it a 99% chance of being right. The rest should be buried somewhere at the old forts if you can find them and if the area has not been disturbed. Landmarks used by the original person who buried the gold long ago may no longer be there. You know it has been two and a half centuries since this story began.”

"Yes, a great amount of time has passed, and yes, I am aware many things have changed. You have given me the basic information I need, but I need more. We need to meet face to face. You can give me the details when we get together. How about tomorrow, the earlier, the better?"

Tom swallowed hard. “Okay, where and what time?” Soon he would be expendable once he told what he knew.

“How about at ten minutes after six tomorrow morning and there is a place near you, Linda’s Old Furnace Restaurant. Could you meet me at that location? Would this work for you?”

"Well, yeah. I could be there then. How will I know you?"

“I will find you. I know what you look like.”

Tom gulped. *Yeah, and I wish I knew what you look like.* “Okay, that’ll work. I can meet you before the workday starts. How long do you think this will take?”

"Oh, not long, but we could have breakfast and talk if you like."

Short? Like a bullet to the head? "I think I'd like the latter. Are you buying?"

"Most definitely. I will drop the dime for your hot. I look forward to meeting you then. Tomorrow just after six at Linda's. See you then."

The phone went dead. The dial tone hissed in Tom's ear. How was this going to go? Drop the dime for my hot? Was the Benefactor trying to tell him something? 'Drop the dime?' Was he coming to betray Tom? And what about the 'for your hot?' What did he mean? A hot was prison talk for a meal. Tom didn't like the sound of this. Maybe, he was paranoid, but people had been trying to kill him. Perhaps, it meant nothing more than he could see at face value. His guts churned at the thought. It was coming to an end, and he had to play with the cards he had even if he wasn't sure about the rules to the game. Tomorrow, he'd meet his nemesis. Tomorrow, he may die. Or maybe not. The clock was ticking down quickly.

Chapter 34

The next morning

The old man arrived at ten minutes to six at Linda's Restaurant in his dark almost black large SUV. He parked very near the entrance, so only a small area of the driver's side was visible from behind the counter where the employees were. Most of the people were still sleeping or rising from bed in the Old Furnace area, but he was sure the employees, cooks, and other helpers, had been at the restaurant several hours before preparing for the breakfast crowd. He was going to miss the area with all its history like the old iron furnace he had just passed no more than a quarter-mile from where he sat. As he pondered his future, he wondered if it would work out as planned or not. The die had been cast. There was no turning back, and he would have it no other way.

Through a large plate glass window, he saw the interior lights come on. A woman walked to the front door and unlocked it. She turned on the bright red neon OPEN sign. It was officially time for business. The SUV's windows were heavily tinted. He could see out, but no one could tell he was in the vehicle from the outside. He opened the car door, went inside the restaurant, and took a seat in the far corner. His back was to the wall, and no one could come toward him without being seen.

A waitress he recognized came to his table and after a short conversation, scribbled the order on her pad. She took it to the cook, who took one look and went to work at the stove. The waitress returned to the old man with two large cups of steaming coffee. He thanked her and took a sip. Just as he liked it, almost hot enough to burn. Now there was nothing left to do but wait for Mr. Kenney. He suspected he would be on time, maybe even a little early.

Several other patrons arrived at the establishment. One sat at the bar stools, one got a carryout in a white Styrofoam container and left, and one took a table near the front windows. The door opened again, and Tom Kenney walked in on high alert. Every eye in the restaurant turned to him except the old man. Quickly, they went back to reading the *Cumberland Times-News* Linda made available each morning. Tom looked the place over closely and recognized only the old man.

He walked to him. “Hello, Mr. Godfrey. What are you doing here? You’re a welcome surprise. I’m planning on meeting someone this morning.”

“What a coincidence. I’m here for the same reason.”

"Have you ordered? Breakfast is excellent, lots of variety from cereals to eggs, and anything else you want, and you can get it all day long if you like.”

“Thank you, Mr. Kenney. I did not know that. Oh, I took the liberty of ordering for you. The hot is on my dime today.”

An expression of disbelief came to Tom’s face. “You? I can’t believe it, but I should’ve known.”

“Believe it. I am the one you came to meet today.”

“So, you’re my Benefactor?”

“I am he. I am known by many names, the less you know of them, the better for you.”

Tom thought for a moment. "I believe you 100%. I've seen only an inkling of what you're capable of, and I don't need to know any more."

“You are much better off not knowing. In this case, the more knowledge you have, the more danger you would be in.”

At that time, the waitress appeared with two plates of food and sat them in front of the two men. She swiftly returned, topped off Mr. Godfrey’s coffee cup, and left. “Mr. Kenney, would it be okay if I blessed our meal. I am somewhat new to this, but I do remember some of the teachings from parochial school. Sister Mary Ella would be shocked; I am certain. I want to do it. Because of you, I gave my life to the Lord.”

"That's great news. You made my day."

“I can’t thank you enough. Now, may I pray?”

“Please do. Practice makes perfect, I’m told.”

“Almighty God, bless this morning meal to our hungry bodies. Dear Lord, my Savior, it is so good to address you as so. I had everything, and yet I had nothing. I gave up nothing I can hold onto and gained everything. You paid the price for my sins and soul. You said ‘Tetelestai, it is finished, paid in full,’ and I thank you for my new life now and forever. Amen.” A tear flowed from his eye.

“Amen,” Tom said. He was quiet for several seconds. “Mr. Godfrey, you spoke from your heart. Keep Him in your heart and follow Him to your last breath. I can give you no better advice in your new walk. Just keep on keepin’ on. What do you say we eat? Smellin’ this great food has made me powerful hungry. Let's eat, and we'll talk afterward if that’s okay with you?”

“Agreed. Eat up, as they commonly say in these parts.”

The two men chowed down on the meal between many sips of the elixir of life, commonly known as coffee. Mr. Godfrey finished first. He wiped his mouth with a paper napkin and said, "Thank you for never giving up on me changing. I thought my case was hopeless, and my sentence was death with no chance of clemency, but you showed me Jesus could give me an unconditional pardon and restore me like nothing had happened."

“Yes, He expunged your record forever. No evidence remains against you. His love cleaned your scarlet stains white as newly fallen snow. It’s like it never happened. Only He can do that for us.”

“Most people would have given up on me, but you did not. I do not know how to thank you. I said I wanted you to tell me of the treasure you knew about, and you did. That treasure was far greater than Braddock’s Gold, or all the gold in this world is worth. You showed me something eternal no thief can steal.”

“You’re so right about that. And speaking of Braddock’s Gold, what about it, Mr. Godfrey?”

“Let us compare notes. See if our conclusions are the same or similar. I believe it was recovered and was reburied in several places not too far from where we sit presently.”

Tom nodded, and Mr. Godfrey continued, "I believe at least half of the original treasure has been lost or spent some time in the last 250 years. The rest was buried at three of the nearby French & Indian War era forts George Washington ordered built- Fort Nichols, Fort Sellers, and Fort Cocke.”

He continued, “No one knows precisely where the latter one is today. Many guesses have been made, but it’s been lost to the sands of time. The Fort Nichols cache has also disappeared, and the one at Fort Sellers is the only one remaining."

Tom said, "There's one more cache. A small box of old gold coins turned up during some digging near the town of Fort Ashby. It's currently in a safe deposit box at a bank waiting for a decision as to its fate."

“Interesting. I did not know that. I have no more to add. Do you have any more, Mr. Kenney?”

“No, that sums it up nicely. That’s my complete knowledge on the whereabouts of Braddock’s Gold.”

“There is one more matter, Mr. Kenney.”

“Let me guess. We’re going Dutch?”

Mr. Godfrey smiled. “No, Mr. Kenney. After all you have done for me, I most certainly will pay for our meal. No, it’s something much more important. You see, I must go away. This may very well be the last time I see you. I cannot and will not explain myself other than to say I must transform.”

“Transform? That’s pretty vague. Can’t you be a little more specific?”

“No. You need to leave it alone. Perhaps, sometime in the future, you may understand. It is best; I say no more. Let it go at that.”

“I guess I don’t have much choice.”

“Trust me, Mr. Kenney. I will not forget you and will see you are taken care of as I promised.”

“That’s good to know. Do you have anything more you need to tell me before we go?”

“No, Mr. Kenney. Just good luck to you and yours, and God bless you. Thank you for having the courage to keep sharing the Gospel to me until it finally sank in. I guess we need to be going. I have plans I need to finalize, and I am certain you have a company to run. Time and tide wait for no one, not even newspaper magnates or small business owners. I need to make several phone calls. I can do so here, and I am sure our waitress will continue to fill my cup in exchange for a large tip. It is all good, Mr. Kenney. Have a great time. Till we meet again here or on the other side.”

"I'm so glad this meeting went as it did. I thought maybe I was walking into an ambush today. Whatever your plans, I hope and pray they work out."

“Likewise, I am sure.”

Tom extended his hand to Mr. Godfrey, and they shook. "Goodbye, Mr. Kenney. May peace be with you.”

“And you too, Mr. Godfrey. Till we meet again.”

Tom got up and exited the restaurant. The young waitress came and refilled his coffee cup. “Thank you,” he said.

“You’re welcome,” she said with a smile, walked away, and refilled other customers’ cups.

It had better work out. Some people could die if it does not, and some people could die if it does. There has been enough death already.

He would do all in his power to see no one died, but one thing he’d learned numerous times in his life; he could not see the future clearly, not even with all the power and influence he had. He wasn’t all-powerful. Some things were beyond his control.

Chapter 35

Tom pulled his new truck into the parking lot at Linda's just after 7 o'clock one week later. His old Chevy had died again, and repairing it would be counterproductive. Repair costs as of late have gone up like a rocket, and he had decided it was best to scrap his old faithful Chevy truck. The new vehicle had a crew cab, a long bed, heavy-duty suspension, and was a dually. He could use it for work if he needed, and most likely, he would.

He walked in the front door, and every head turned to see who it was. Linda was sitting on a barstool near the kitchen reading today's newspaper and nursing a cup of coffee. A half-eaten doughnut sat on a small plate next to her. Seeing Tom, she said, "Hey, Tom. Have you seen the news?"

"No, I haven't. What's up?"

"You need to see this."

He sat down on the barstool next to her, and she handed him the front section of today's *Cumberland Times-News* with the front page up. The double sized and bold headline read **Newspaper Magnate's Jet Crashes, All Aboard Believed Dead.**

Below the headline was a large headshot of Mr. Godfrey and another picture of him standing next to a Learjet. The article by Suanne Bishop-Long started at the fold in the middle of the page. It began, "Yesterday afternoon at 3:44 pm EDT, a plane piloted by the owner of the *Cumberland Times-News* and the Geoffrey Transnational Consortium, Mr. Gino Godfrey, crashed in the Caribbean Sea off the coast of Puerto Rico. He was believed to be on a humanitarian mission to an undisclosed Central American country. Five people were believed on board the aircraft.

"The plane, known as the Phoenix, left Cumberland Municipal Airport, located in Wiley Ford, West Virginia early in the morning. It made an unscheduled stop at Ti-Co Airport near Kennedy Space Center in Florida and also in the Cayman Islands for undisclosed problems. The last communication received was at 2:02 pm EDT. Shortly afterward, the plane made a left turn, possibly the result of human input. A thunderstorm was in the area. At 2:15 pm EDT, the aircraft didn't respond to a call for a change in radio frequencies. No additional attempts to contact the pilot were successful.

"The plane was believed to be on autopilot and angled off course. U.S. Air Force jets scrabbled from Eglin Air Force Base in Florida and Howard Air Base in Panama. The first to arrive observed heavy condensation or frost on the windshield. Early reports state the belief that the plane lost cabin pressure. No motion was seen through a small clear patch on the windshield. Shortly following this observation, the aircraft began a rapid ascent skyward, caught fire, and then began a near-vertical descent where it crashed into the Caribbean Sea. Very little debris was observed as well as no survivors. No effort was planned for recovery of any remaining parts of the plane. The area in the Puerto Rico Trench where the crash occurred is five miles deep or more.

“National Transportation Safety Board (NTSB) speculated it is likely the aircraft had a loss of cabin pressure. All on board would have lost consciousness shortly after leaving the Cayman Islands. Occupants would have only a few brief seconds to don oxygen masks before cognitive and motor skill would be impaired. Anyone aboard would have been incapacitated very shortly afterward, followed by death. NTSB records show the aircraft had several entries concerning maintenance work related to cabin pressure recently.

“Authorities are attempting to identify the other passengers in the private aircraft to notify next of kin. Funeral arrangements are incomplete at this time. Condolences can be sent to the following address: *Cumberland Times-News*, Baltimore Avenue, Cumberland, Maryland, 21502."

Tom looked at Linda. “I don’t know what to say. I’m shocked.”

She said, “Me, too. Didn’t you have breakfast with him right here about a week ago?”

“I sure did. He gave me some important news and told me he was going away, but I don’t think this was what he was referring to. I don’t know what to say.”

"Tom, you and I both know there's no guarantee for tomorrow. Here today, gone tomorrow. The Lord gives, and He takes away."

“Blessed be the name of the Lord. Linda, the personal thing he told me was he had given his life to the Lord. At least we know where he is now.”

“Amen to that, Tom. Are you still looking for breakfast?”

"I've kinda lost my appetite, but why don't you fix up a number one? Maybe I'll be hungry later."

"How you want your eggs cooked?"

"Scrambled and with bacon today."

"Homefries or sliced potatoes?

"Homefries."

"White or wheat bread?"

"Wheat."

"Toasted or not?"

"Toasted with jelly. Any more questions?"

"Grape or strawberry?"

"Linda, you're gonna drive me crazy with questions. Please, no more."

She smiled, "Cash, credit or debit?"

"Cash and get me a coffee to go. Black, no sugar or cream or flavorings, please.

She continued to smile, "Regular or decaf?"

"Linda, you know how I like my coffee."

"I know, but it was fun to mess with you. I think we could all use a little humor right now."

"Yeah, I guess we could. It's hard to believe he's gone."

"Yes, it is. He stopped in for a meal now and then. I think he had a place near here."

"Yeah, I believe he did."

“I’ll whip up your meal. It looks like Lois is busy with orders. It’ll take me, oh, no more than ten minutes max. Is that good?”

“That’s good. Took ten minutes for you to take my order.”

She smiled, "I'll get it for you now.” She disappeared into the kitchen.

Tom sat at the stool by the bar and looked at the funnies, but he saw nothing funny today. A man he knew too well and yet barely knew had died. He’d regretted ever meeting him, and yet, he was glad he’d been a positive influence on him. God sure works in mysterious ways.

Chapter 36

Big Tony sat at his desk at Ned's Bar in Hagerstown, Maryland, and couldn't believe what he was reading in today's paper, Mr. Godfrey, the Boss, dead? How could that be? He'd just seen him and to die in something as senseless as a mechanical problem in his aircraft, the Phoenix?

He knew all the people who were with the Boss. He didn't need to wait for the investigators to find out and report this to the public. He knew beyond the shadow of a doubt. The old man was finally dead, but was he? Mr. Godfrey was a man of many overt and covert talents, but was he really dead? No man could escape the Grim Reaper, not ever the Boss, but still, he wondered.

Just yesterday, he had another huge surprise. An ordinary-looking manila envelope arrived in the afternoon mail. It had no return address, which wasn't unusual in his line of work. It was sealed very well to make it tamperproof. If anyone had opened it before him, he would have known.

The envelope contained a handwritten letter and a deed. The note read, "Tony, continue business as usual in my absence. I have to go away for an extended period. I will be monitoring activates from a distant place. Don't try to locate me or follow my whereabouts. I will be perfectly safe and at rest. My final destination is not your concern. Stay the course, and don't disappoint me. You know I don't take disappointment well. If I have to interrupt my time away, it won't go well. Be happy with what you have and enjoy your new-found wealth. Those who sow the wind will reap the whirlwind. Till we meet again. G. G."

G.G., a.k.a. Gino Godfrey. The Boss rarely signed anything traceable back to him. He meant this to be very secure and personal. The deed was signed and official. The Boss had given him the establishment known as Ned's Place, lock, stock, and barrel. He owned this place free and clear. He was set for life. He could kick back and enjoy the fruits it produced and live the good life. But what about Braddock's Gold? He knew for sure where at least one cache was. It had to be worth a minimum of a quarter-million dollars. Was it worth the price he could pay or not? What about Braddock's Gold?

***

That same day, Pan-American Highway, Honduras-Nicaragua border

The dark blue-black Chevy Impala sedan pulled up to a border crossing late that night, shortly before 11 p.m. The car had heavily tinted glass all around, and it was difficult for the border guard to see who was in the vehicle. He motioned for the driver to roll down the window, which he did. After a few questions in Spanish, five passports were produced, and each one contained an American $100 bill sticking out. He pocketed three of the bills, walked into a small building, and handed the passports, and $200 to the immigration man sitting at the desk. The second man pocketed the money, quickly stamped the passports, and returned them to the border guard. Neither man spoke. Nothing needed to be said. It was all in a night's work. One hundred dollars was a month's pay for either man. It was business as usual.

The guard handed the passports to the driver and told him to proceed and drive carefully. Thieves had stolen some of the road signs, and they could come upon a sharp and dangerous turn unaware. The driver thanked him and proceeded down the road. As the guard watched the taillights disappear, he realized the one man looked familiar. He wondered if he should say something. Could it be him? He put his hand in his pants pocket and felt the three $100 bills. No, he didn’t want to know that badly.

***

At the villa known as the Compound near Jinotepe, Nicaragua

It had been three weeks now that the old man had been in the country at his new home and he was enjoying himself. His Spanish was improving as each day went by. The people were happy to finally see the man whose generosity had established and funded the clinic on the Compound for decades. They had begun to call him Señor Amado, Mr. Beloved, which he rather liked. However, things back home troubled him. From his office in the inner sanctum of the Compound, he could monitor any electronic communications anywhere in the world and see any location in real-time. The locals paid little attention to the vast array of tall towers on the hill behind the Compound. Most thought the government owned them. The information he was receiving was starting to form a picture, one he didn't like. A decision would have to be made soon, very soon.

Chapter 37

Tom walked out of Wayne's Grocery in Fort Ashby, West Virginia, carrying a fat check. Wayne's was his first account, and his brand, Knobley Mountain Bottled Water, was now the bestselling of its kind at Wayne's two stores. His business was booming. He'd turned down several lucrative offers from big-name companies to buy him out, and it seemed the trouble that had dogged him for several years was finally behind him. He had met the nemesis who called himself the Benefactor and had survived. The curse of Braddock's Gold was behind him. No more would someone threaten him or try to kill him over the treasure. The Benefactor assured Tom he would see no harm came to him.

He walked to his new crew cab truck he had used to deliver the pallet of water to the grocery store. Funny, he thought he'd locked it, but never mind. It was an oversight. His wife, Joann, had been chiding him lately about his absentmindedness. Tom hopped in and started it up. He loved the sound of its mighty V8 rumbling. Washington Street was nice and smooth since the repaving. He took a left on WV 28 and headed toward his house and left the business behind. The water in Patterson Creek was running low again; he noted as he crossed the bridge. The feel of cold steel on his neck got his attention.

“What’s going on?” he said. “Is this a robbery? Do you want my truck? You can have it.”

“Shut up and drive,” demanded the steely voice.

Tom looked in the rearview mirror and saw a big man wearing a ski mask. “What do you want?”

“I want you to take the next road to the right and shut up. I’ll do the talking.”

Tom did as he was told. He turned onto Patterson Creek Road. There was something familiar about the voice, but he couldn’t place it. He drove the bumpy secondary road to the sleepy little town of Patterson Creek. "Take the next right," the mask snarled, and Tom did.

“We’re going to the old farm up on the ridge, aren’t we?” Tom said.

“You’re a smart fellow, and you, Mr. Smarty Pants, are going to make me a rich man. You’re going to show me where Braddock’s gold is. Capisce?”

“Yes, I understand.”

Now that he knew his destination, there was no further need for direction. Tom took a right at Dans Run Road, passed over the old railroad tracks, then over the low water bridge, up the steep hill, and onto the side road leading up to the old farmhouse and the site of Fort Sellers, the last known location of the gold payroll of General Braddock. A gate blocked the way.

"Ram the gate and keep moving," the man growled. Tom did as instructed, and the gate tore apart as he drove through it. "See? That was easy. Keep it up, and you might live."

Fat chance of that, Tom thought, but he prayed for a way out.

“Pull up to the house and get out. You’ll find the shovel in the back of your truck. You know where to dig.”

Tom did as he was told. He walked the short distance to the hole he'd been digging when first shot because of Braddock's gold. Was this to be a repeat of that incidence? Would this be his grave also?

He looked in the hole and saw it was bigger and deeper than he remembered. Tom said nothing and began to dig at the bottom of the six-foot deep hole. After working for ten minutes, he wiped his brow and said, "I could use some help down here."

The mask grinned sardonically, and grunted, “Dig if you know what’s good for you and do it faster.” The masked man looked around. He heard something, and Tom heard it too, but he wasn't sure what it was. Yes, it was a helicopter, one like he'd never seen or heard, and it hovered a thousand feet away. "No," the mask said, "It can't be." And then his head exploded.

Tom dropped to the bottom of the hole. A few moments later, the black helicopter approached and hovered over the hole. Tom could see an M240 machine gun sticking out one side and a smaller gun with a long barrel protruding from the other. It moved slowly away and sat down very close. He could feel the wind from the five-blade rotor. “Get out of the hole, Mr. Kenney,” someone demanded.

Tom knew there was no way to escape. He stood expecting a shot, but none came. Slowly he crawled out of the hole and held his hands up. Five men were on the ground. All wore dark camo clothing from neck to toe, and they wore tactical combat masks over their heads. One more man, the pilot, remained in the ready chopper. The four men hastily put the headless corpse in a body bag and carried it to the helicopter. They got in. The man remaining on the ground motioned for them to leave, and the bird lifted off. It quickly disappeared, leaving Tom alone with the man who carried a wicked-looking long rifle. He was of medium to short stature and seemed a little out of place. Tom and the man stared at each other.

"What's the matter? Don't you recognize me?" the man said.

"The voice sounds vaguely familiar. Who are you?"

"Perhaps I should have used my altered voice, Mr. Tom Kenney. Maybe then you would know me."

"Mr. Godfrey? It can't be you. You're…."

"Dead? I assure you I'm very much alive." He took off the mask. "I'll soon leave and rejoin the dearly departed. Nothing happened here today."

"Who was the man you killed?"

"Big Tony. He knew you from the prison when you did chaplain work, and he was here when the young, drugged-out tweaker threatened you on this very spot and was shot and killed. Tony wouldn't have let you live."

"But how did you know?"

"Let's say many bigger men than Tony have underestimated me and regretted it. How I know isn't important. The important thing is I promised to keep you safe. Sadly, someone had to die to do that. As far as I know, Tony was the last threat to you concerning Braddock's gold."

"Thank you for watching over me from afar. Just curious, what kind of helicopter was that?"

"Officially, it doesn't exist. Let's call it a Comanche, and you're to forget you ever saw it."

"I can do that."

"There's something else, Tom. Haven't you noticed? You're not in PTSD shock. Don't you usually have one of those episodes after a traumatic event?"

"You're right. I do, but not today. Maybe, just maybe, I'm over it."

"I can't talk long, Mr. Kenney. As I said, I need to disappear again. I was never here."

Tom nodded, "I guess I'd better leave too. Gonna be hard to explain the damaged truck."

"Take it to Jump's Auto Repair. I'll see it gets fixed and at no cost to you."

"Thank you, Mr. Godfrey." Tom stuck out his hand, but the old man embraced him.

They separated, and Tom walked to his truck. As he slowly drove away, he saw Mr. Godfrey waving his hand. A black helicopter landed. It quickly departed at high speed with the old man on board. Tom neared the crumbled gate. A deer with a magnificent rack stood in the road. Tom stopped ten feet away from it and blared the horn. The buck bounded away rapidly and was soon out of sight.

Jump's drove Tom home and fixed his truck at no cost to him.

The state confiscated the old farm where they grew the marijuana. The adjoining property owned by Mr. Godfrey was given to the state of West Virginia as directed in his will. He specified its use as a state park or state preserve whatever worked out best for the new owner.

A mob war broke out up and down the East Coast's major metropolitan region that started in Boston and ended in Richmond. Numerous men died or disappeared over the upcoming months, and it only stopped when the US Attorney General, US Marshals Service, the FBI, and several other federal law enforcement departments became heavily involved. Many speculated they had waited to intervene until after the various factions were heavily weakened, which was what the feds wanted all along. Big Tony's vanishing was attributed to mob violence.

Tom and Joann were not able to have any more children. Their little girl, Brook, grew up, tall and slim. They adopted twins from the Navajo Reservation in Arizona, and the boys played with the grandkids Tom's married sons and daughters-in-law produced.

Daughter Miriah grew up and became a veterinarian. Tom sold a 49% interest in his company to his son, Doug. Tom bought a place in Florida, and the family would use it when they wanted. He later sold his remaining interest in the company to Doug, who continued to build it bigger. The big boys in the business kept trying to buy out Knobley Mountain Bottled Water, but Doug refused to sell his little gold mine of a company.

The gold found at the Berean Church was sold to dealers and brought just shy of $200,000. The deacons of the church voted to split the money with Dan Phares. His share was put in a trust and invested in a growing portfolio by a slick young financial advisor named Ron Strawder at First People's Federal Credit Union. Dan never worried about having money again.

Dutch, who discovered the gold at the church, found it was more profitable for him to contract his own work than wait on a job through the union. The company he started, CES Excavating, became one of the largest in the county over the next decade.

Father Frank, aka Padre, became a member of the Pittsburgh Police Department. He served as officer, chaplain, and head of the local Boy's Club in the inner city. He received several distinguished citations for his service, one for bravery when he rescued a woman and her two children from a house fire on a freezing winter's night.

One of his two sons got a Ph.D. in Engineering and went to work for Westinghouse Electric. The other played football at West Virginia University and later for the Pittsburgh Steelers. Frank never missed a game. He was proud of both of them, who became role models for the black community.

Shortly before Padre retired, his wife died in an auto accident involving an illegal alien gang member on the run from several state and federal agencies. Though the criminal wanted for two murders survived the crash in downtown Pittsburgh's Golden Triangle area, he died in a gun battle trying to escape.

Frank made many calls to Tom Kenney, who helped him through this difficult time. All too well, Tom remembered and could relate to losing a spouse in an auto crash. Frank never remarried and went back into the priesthood.

And with all the kids and grandkids around, Tom could not afford to grow old, though he did eventually, but not before having many more adventures.

The End

Isaiah 9:2 The people walking in darkness have seen a great light; a light has dawned on those living in the land of darkness.

WANT TO READ MORE?

Braddock's Gold Mystery Series

Braddock's Gold

Hunter's Moon

Fool's Wisdom

Killing Darkness

Florida Murder Mystery Series

Death at Windover

Murder at the Canaveral Diner

Murder at the Indian River

WANT TO HELP THE AUTHOR?

If you enjoyed the book, would you help get the word out? Please tell others about it. Word-of-mouth advertising is the best marketing tool on this planet.

A review on Amazon, Goodreads, or elsewhere would help with the author being able to keep writing full time. It doesn't have to be long. Thanks.

SIGN UP FOR JAY HEAVNER'S NEWSLETTER

With this, Jay will occasionally keep you informed with new books coming out and anything else special. Feel free to email him at jay@jayheavner.com. His website is https://jayheavner.com. He loves reader feedback.

www.ingramcontent.com/pod-product-compliance
Lightning Source LLC
Chambersburg PA
CBHW060629260626
47161CB00008B/2838
9781733617468